THE FAR HC

Gretta Curran Browne

SPI

Seanelle Publications Inc.

ISBN: 978-1-912598-63-2

Cover: Melody Simmons

AUTHOR'S NOTE

Although presented here as a novel, and cloaked in the style of fiction, this story is a true one based on the letters, diaries and documents of Lachlan Macquarie, Elizabeth Campbell, and many of the other people involved.

For providing me with copies from microfilm of relevant documents from the Macquarie Papers, I am deeply grateful to the Mitchell Library in Sydney, as well as to the Archives Authority of New South Wales.

TO

My beloved Ellena

who now lives beyond that far horizon

PART ONE

Chapter One

The college for young men in Edinburgh was private, prestigious and expensive. Scotland's Oxford, some called it. The grounds leading up to the beautiful grey-stone Georgian building were covered in neatly trimmed green lawns and shaded by massive fir trees. Above its halls and classrooms, young men sat in their private rooms studying every subject from Mathematics to Latin.

On this March morning in May 1808, Drew Alexander sat sloped over his desk in a long lazy daydream; one of his many daydreams about his hero, so distant and aloof in many ways, yet so kind and helpful, and so astonishingly beautiful.

Outside, after one of the fiercest winters Scotland had ever known, the sunshine was unfolding into a mild and bright day, so mild and dry that Drew wondered if perhaps he could persuade his hero to take a walk outside with him, perhaps up to the crags to see if they could spot an eagle. Any excuse would do. Just the thought of the two of them walking together, alone; talking together, alone; made his heart beat a little faster. At eighteen, his earlier fascination had now become so consumable that Drew could rarely think of anything or anyone else.

The door flew open and O'Keefe walked in. 'I say, Drew, is your friend George leaving us? I just saw him rushing down the stairs carrying a portmanteau.'

'Leaving?'

The blood rushed into Drew's cheeks and for a moment he could not speak; then a moment later he was up on his feet and rushing out to the stairs, scattering down them so fast he skidded at the bottom and had to quickly recover himself – but then he was at the front door, staring after the tall young man in a dark blue fitted jacket, showing the firm strong lines of his graceful body, his clean black hair gleaming in the sunshine.

Unable to stop himself, Drew hurtled down the path, calling frantically: 'George! George!'

George looked back, and then raised his hand in a quick sign to Drew that he must hurry, could not delay.

A moment later Drew was beside George asking in a breathless voice where he was going. 'You're not leaving us, George, are you?'

'No, no.' George briefly smiled his wonderful smile. 'I need to visit my father.'

'Your father?' Drew still did not know exactly just *who* George's father was. It could not be the man who occasionally came to visit him here, because his name was Macquarie and he was far too young. A tall and fair-haired man, a soldier, an officer in His Majesty's army who sometimes arrived still wearing the scarlet jacket of his uniform and at other times dressed elegantly civilian – but George was now twenty, and that man was aged only in his late-thirties at the most.

Apart from that, Mr Macquarie was Scottish and white, and George's skin was smooth and light brown, like a Spaniard, definitely of foreign blood. But there was so much mystery surrounding George, so much that he refused to discuss, so much that Drew longed to know.

Drew suddenly felt the chill in the air and began to shiver. The sunshine outside his window had misled him – it was still bitterly cold. Yet despite the cold, he noticed that George carried his navy wool cloak over his arm, and had the impatient air of a man who had packed hastily.

'How long will you be gone?'

'A week, two weeks, a year – however long my father needs me,' George said impatiently, 'but I must go now.'

Drew suddenly grabbed George's hand in a terrible clasp, wanting to tell him how much he would miss him, fighting back tears in case it showed weakness, which he was sure George would dislike, because despite his beautifully handsome looks, George also had a mature masculinity which so many of the other young men at the school lacked.

George gently withdrew his hand from Drew's grip, eager to get away from the hurt expression in his friend's eyes. He had long been conscious of Drew's feelings for him, but there was nothing he could do to help him, except to avoid him as much as possible. Of course, he was very young, much younger than his eighteen years, so hopefully his schoolboy obsession would disappear with time.

Half an hour later George boarded the Mail-coach. He sat back and looked around at his fellow passengers: an old man pretending to be asleep; a plump matronly woman hungrily eating a fried sausage; a young man reading a book, and a man of middle years with long flowing hair and wearing a red plaid cape who, as soon as the coach started rolling, commenced to entertain his fellow-passengers with a few "gleg" jokes he had recently heard.

Many of the jokes, with their Scottish nuances, George did not understand, but others he did and smiled occasionally, if only in polite response to the comedic man who was working so hard to entertain them on their journey.

Finally he grew tired of it all and turned to gaze out of the window, his mind darkening with the shadows of his thoughts, wondering why Elizabeth had sent for him so urgently.

*

George was so lost in the distance of his thoughts, he was unaware that the young man sitting opposite had lowered his book, and had been studying him carefully for some time, taking in the fine quality of the clothes he wore and the refinement of his manners since he had entered the coach. And then, of course, there was the colour of his skin, which reminded the young man of some paintings he had recently seen of those red

Indians in America; except those red Indians in America had not looked red at all, but light brown, just like the young man sitting opposite. There was also something very familiar about him.

'You'll aye pardon me for asking, sir,' said the young man finally in a curious tone. 'Are you ... Scaw'ish?'

George blinked, and looked at his fellow passenger with a slight smile. 'No, I am not Scottish.'

'Are you, then ... a visitor?'

'A visitor to where?'

'To Scawtland.'

George could see that he now had the attention of the other passengers who were listening avidly.

'No,' he admitted honestly, 'I am not a visitor. I am a resident.'

'Aye, of Edinburgh?'

'Of Edinburgh,' George confirmed.

'Are you a personage of some sort? You have the bearing and manners of a personage of quality.'

George was quite confident that he was indeed a person of quality, but perhaps not quite in the way his fellow passenger meant.

'I feel I must know you,' the young man persisted, betraying his own lack of manners. 'I believe that at some time we musta had your custom.'

'Custom?' George was not only perplexed, but was now becoming slightly irritated with the inquisitive young man opposite.

'Aye,' replied the young man, pointing to George's jacket. We are the only "Gentlemen's Outfitters" in the whole of Scawtland that supplies that particular yarn of cloth. I would know it anywhere. Finest you'll see this side of London.'

'Ah.' George finally understood. 'You are employed at Mortimers?'

'Aye, I'm one of the tailors, and I've admired that particular yarn of cloth for a long time now, blended with cashmere as it is. That's why it's warm but not too heavy, the fine thread of the wool. Aye, indeed, a gleg cloth – one of our best.'

George nodded in agreement. 'My father introduced me to Mortimers. He believes they are the finest tailors in Edinburgh.'

'And you?'

'Oh, I too believe they are the finest.'

Two red spots suddenly coloured the young man's cheeks. 'Aye, the best ... and it's my own fond ambition to become the top tailor at Mortimers one day; the head of the workroom.'

'I'm sure you will,' George smiled. 'Especially if you had anything to do with the excellent making of this jacket.'

'Aye, I did, sir, it's one of mine. I recognised it after I had taken a good look at it, after you sat down.' He leaned forward to touch the double-breasted lapels on George's blue jacket. 'You see the cut of the corners on the lapels here, sir? I have my own particular way of cutting them, and, aye – that's one of mine.'

George was not sure what further compliment he should offer the young tailor, who gave him no chance to say anything.

'And – erm ... could I know your name, sir? Seeing as you're wearing one of my own creations. It would be nice to know.'

'Jarvis,' George replied. 'George Jarvis.'

The other passengers, who had been following the conversation, stared at George and then exchanged wide-eyed expressive glances with each other as if to say now *that* was unexpected – such a very *English* name for one who looked so foreign.

The coach suddenly jolted violently over some large holes in the dirt road and everyone sat back firmly in their seats, giving George the moment to turn away from their curious stares and end all conversation by gazing out at the bleak scenery; and then closing his eyes as if wishing to sleep – tired of being a subject of curiosity – something he had always been in this land from the first day he had landed on the shores of *Belait,* or 'Blighty' as the English so badly pronounced it.

*

He was an Arabic Indian, born in the Palace of Surat. His mother had been a beautiful young Moroccan girl, snatched at the age of fourteen from a crowded and noisy street in Tangiers and sold into the slave trade.

His father was one of the many young princes in the palace at Surat who had yelped with delight when he laid eyes on the exquisite young girl who was to be his new concubine; and the fact that she did not understand *gujerati,* and therefore not one word he said to her, made her even more delectable to him.

Their son was born one year later, when his mother was barely fifteen years old.

George had no idea what his real name was, as his mother had always called him her *'amir'* – her prince. It was the only thing she was proud of, highly proud, that her son's father was a royal prince, albeit of a foreign land and foreign race.

And the prince had looked after them both well, making sure they had the best of everything. George had sketchy memories of his early childhood, none at all until he was aged about five years old, but from that age he had recollections of the kind and lovely Indian *ayahs* who took turns in looking after him; and the jasmine-scented garden he played in, with its high stone walls shading out the fiercest heat of the mid-day sun.

He also still remembered the golden silk of the large cushions he slept on; and *always* ... always his mother's arms clasped tightly around him, whispering to him about the land she had come from – the land and family she longed to return to ... somehow, some way ... *'Morocco ... Morocco...'*

After six years of her company, the royal prince decided he had suffered enough of her homesickness and had also grown tired of her. He had a beautiful new concubine to replace her now, so she could go back to Morocco and stay there – but not the boy! The boy was his. She could not take him, not to Morocco, not even outside the palace walls.

All this, his mother had told him later, after one of the *ayahs,* a concubine who had become her special friend over the years, had helped her to smuggle her *'prince'* out of the palace and live on the run from all searchers; hiding here and hiding there, travelling across India like a tramp, begging food for herself and her child. And always so desperate to find her way home to the family she had been stolen from seven years earlier.

But she never did find her way home. They had both been captured near the coast road to Bombay by a group of Dutch slave-traders who hauled them aboard a cart, and then a ship, and then sold them to a Dutch slave-trader at the southern port of Cochin – almost a thousand miles away from Surat – and forever away from Morocco.

*

George was eventually brought out of his thoughts by a hand touching his arm. He blinked, and then looked round to see the young tailor smiling at him, his hand held out.

'It's been a pleasure to meet you, sir, and I hope Mortimers will have the benefit of your custom again.'

The coach had stopped. George had not even been aware of its sudden cease of motion. He nodded at the tailor with a brief smile. 'Yes, you will,' he said amiably, and shook the tailor's hand in farewell.

The other passengers had collected their bits and pieces and were climbing down from the coach. George waited until the carriage was empty and then followed them out, stepping down to be greeted by a sharp wind, gusty and hostile.

He quickly draped his cloak around him, collected his portmanteau from the driver, then without delaying to take any refreshment inside the coach house, he bent his head against the wind and immediately set off on the two-mile walk to the military base, his mind constantly focused on the dark fear that something bad had happened to the beloved man who had rescued him from the slave trade all those years ago in Cochin, the beloved man he always referred to as 'father' in the respectful tradition of the East, and not the paternal tradition of the West; although, in George's heart and mind, Lachlan was both.

*

The house was less than a mile outside the main barracks. Darkness had fallen by the time George reached it, but only one of the front windows glowed with light. Usually they were all aglow, cheerful and welcoming, but not tonight. Yes, something was wrong ... very wrong. The urgency of Elizabeth's summons spurred him faster to the front door.

The housekeeper answered his knock, holding up a lamp to peer at him. 'Ah, it's ye at last George ...' she said in a tone of relief. 'Thank God you've come.'

She silently beckoned for him to go into the parlour, the only room with a light on, and there he found Elizabeth sitting alone by the fire, tear-drenched and white-faced and looking as if she had lost a stone in weight.

'Elizabeth?'

As soon as Elizabeth stood to greet him with open arms, more tears flooded down her face as she croaked, 'I thought she was sleeping, George, I – I ... Oh God, I *hate* this place now ...'

'Elizabeth ...' George moved to put his arms around her shoulders to comfort her but she moved him back. 'No, *he* is the one who needs you now, George. You're the only one who will know how to console him ... you've been through this once before with him ... so go, George, now, *please*, upstairs ...'

You've been through this once before with him ... That was the moment George knew what had happened here, and why Elizabeth had so urgently sent for him. The shock, and then the sudden pain inside his chest was so fierce, so terrible, that he could have been physically sick.

'Jane...?' he whispered in disbelief. 'Jane? Oh, no ... no.' He turned and quickly left the room, his quickening footsteps creaking the wooden stairs until he reached the wood-panelled hall that led to the largest bedroom at the back of the house.

Lachlan was sitting in the dark, staring unseeingly at the last few red embers in the fireplace as he held his baby daughter in his arms.

'Lachlan ...'

Lachlan slowly turned his gaze from the fire and looked at George. His was not an easy face for most people to read, but even in the dimness of the firelight, George could see the pain in his eyes, the same pain he had seen in his eyes in Macao in China, when his beloved young wife had died suddenly and without warning; only twenty-three-years old, and she, too, had been named Jane Jarvis Macquarie.

'How?' George whispered.

'Pneumonia ... this damnable winter ... Christ, George; she's only three months old. Is everyone I love to be taken from me so young?'

'You love Elizabeth, and you still have her.'

'Oh, poor Elizabeth ... ' Lachlan momentarily closed his eyes. 'She is suffering, George, in great pain. Will you go and comfort her.'

'No, *you* should go and comfort her,' George said softly. 'Elizabeth is the one who needs you now, not Jane. I will hold Jane.'

After a silence Lachlan nodded, rising carefully to his feet, reluctant to disturb his child, reluctant to let go of her; and then finally placing her little body in George's arms and quickly turning away.

Alone, in the dimness of the room, George held the baby and looked down into her little face, remembering all the times she had gurgled up at him, her tiny hand reaching towards his face; and how her blue eyes would stare up at him, entranced, whenever he softly sang little songs to her.

He gently put his lips to her small cold face and began to weep silent tears. And with his tears came the realisation ... if this was *his* pain now, *his* grief ... how much harder must it be for her two shocked parents downstairs.

*

Three days later, at the funeral of their child, George Jarvis stood silently with Lachlan and Elizabeth as the small casket was prayed over, and then Elizabeth placed a small white flower on the lid, and Lachlan reached out his hand to touch the casket, just one last time.

And then, as George reached to gently touch the casket also, he heard himself whispering the same words he had heard so many times whispered by his own mother when he was a child.

'*Khudaa hafiz.*' God be with you.

Chapter Two

Fourteen months later, while their home in Perthshire lay basking in the warm glow of summer sunshine, Lachlan and Elizabeth sat down to breakfast but George did not appear.

Elizabeth looked at his empty chair, and then up at Mrs Burgess. 'Is George still in bed?'

'No, he was up and out early. He said to keep him some oatcakes warm.'

The housekeeper shook a batch of hot oatcakes onto a plate straight from the griddle-rack. 'An' I said back to him, "O' course I will, George – but only if ye bring me some nice wild flowers back for ma kitchen."' She chuckled as she turned to leave. 'No' that I'm expectin' him to bend down an' pick *me* flowers, mind ... but mebbe he will for Kirsteen, young and bonnie as she is.'

Elizabeth watched the yellow butter melting on the hot oatcake she had cut in half. 'That's the fourth morning this week George has missed breakfast and gone walking for hours,' she said to Lachlan. 'Is there anything wrong?'

'No, it's the sun.' Lachlan was reading his post. 'Coming from a hot country the sunshine is always like a magnet to George, especially after the winter snow and cold spring we've had.'

A mile away George was strolling in the sun, enjoying its warmth and brightness. All around him the land was lush and green, shining and splendid, as happy to see and feel the sunshine as he was. This recent spell of brilliant warm weather, together with the walks that had accompanied it, had helped him to think, to make up his mind about his future.

Relieved now that his studies and busy college days were finished, a new sense of quiet contentment suffused him as he wandered in the warm greenness of the island, the tranquil silence broken only by the occasional cries of the seagulls flying overhead. The air was fresh and sweet and he breathed it deep into his body, deciding to prolong his walk and take the long route back to the house, and with every step feeling even more certain about his decision. Now nothing was more vital than he should tell Lachlan what he wished he to do.

Nevertheless, as he reached a small stream shaded by trees, he paused to gaze down at the water, pure and sparkling, then hunkered down to catch some in his palm and taste it. The cool wetness on his lips took his memory back to those days in the hot Egyptian desert when he had trudged through the sand dreaming of finding even the smallest rivulet of cooling water like this one, but even when he did find a small wet stream in that desert, it was always a mirage that vanished in a blink.

He rose slowly, his vision focused on the sparkling water as he remembered the 77th's long march across the burning desert to the Nile. After

17

marching forty miles from Suez and then twenty miles into the basin of the desert, all their water had gone, and no sign of a well. No water to drink, and no water to cook the food.

And the *heat!* Even the suffocating heat of India in the hot season could never compare to the blinding dry heat of the silent desert. But the torture of the heat was nothing to the craving thirst, a gravely thirst so painful that some of the soldiers began to cry just to lick their own tears.

There was even a time when George thought he might die from the thirst and lack of water in his body, until he remembered an old Arab trick taught to him in his childhood by his mother from Morocco – to carry a small stone in the mouth, gently sucking it to activate the saliva glands which would keep the tongue moist when the thirst was bad.

Quickly he had searched for a stone, and found one, and then passed the trick on to the soldiers. Formation lines were temporarily broken but nobody cared, not even the officers, and within minutes every soldier was searching for his stone, and when they found it, even if it did not quench the craving thirst, it greatly helped to ease the mouth from dryness.

Two days later they had found the first of only two wells in that hundred-mile passage across the Egyptian desert; but by then, the desert had claimed three dead soldiers from the 77th.

Sixteen he had been then, when they had left

India to join other regiments of the British Army to fight the French in the battle for Alexandria. A battle the British had won.

The soldiers of the 77th had been glad to celebrate the victory, glad to get away from the need to fight and the oppression of constant orders from the officers, relaxing in the cool shaded rooms in the houses near the bazaar where beautiful girls were willing to please them in exchange for money.

So many beautiful girls to choose from, but George chose only one.

She was nearer to his age, only seventeen. He could still see her beautiful young face, her soft dark eyes, her slender figure, her gentle smile ... He had stayed with her in her shaded room for many blissful days, and one of those days had been his seventeenth birthday, he was sure of it, and he told her so. She had been exquisite and delicate, like a beautiful flower, and he had never forgotten her or the desert, because one had led to the other.

Still gazing at the rippling water of the stream, he thought he heard a whisper of a sound behind him, and threw a look across his shoulder, surprised to see Kirsteen, the maid from the house, standing there watching him.

He turned and looked at her with part impatience, part wry wonderment. This was not the first or even the third time she had suddenly appeared behind him this week. His eyes took in the fact that she had removed her apron and changed her dress. Her face had been lightly rouged on the cheeks and her brown hair, normally tied back, had now lost its ribbon and was hanging long and loose.

'You are out walking again?' he asked.

She flushed self-consciously. 'No, but Mrs Burgess was wondering where ye were, and why ye were out so long, with your breakfast getting cold an' all. And Mrs Macquarie was asking for ye too.'

'And she asked you to come and find me?'

'No, no ... she didn't ask me ... but I always like to help the mistress.'

'Then I shall head back immediately.'

Kirsteen eagerly moved to follow him, falling into step beside him. 'Back there by the stream,' she asked, 'what were ye thinking so silently?'

George glanced at her with a slight smile. 'What other way is there to think, except in silence.'

She shrugged, undeterred. 'But now ye are not thinking in silence, are ye? So tell me what ye *were* thinking?'

'Nothing that would interest you, Kirsteen.'

'Anything ye say would interest me, George, honestly it would. Is it alreet if I walk beside ye? I'll not be in your way. And if ye prefer it, I'll no' say a word, honestly I won't, I'll just listen.'

George smiled ruefully as Kirsteen walked beside him, talking non-stop, all the way back to the house.

*

Elizabeth was in the garden, walking up and down in a futile attempt to calm her fears.

'You wanted to speak to me?' George asked her.

Elizabeth nodded. 'Yes, George, you know him so well, I need your advice. Only you can help me to understand.'

'You look distressed,' George observed. 'Has something happened?'

'No, no ... not yet at least.' She glanced quickly around her. 'Let's move further away from the house. Kirsteen is always hiding somewhere and listening to my conversations with you.'

When they had reached the far end of the garden she sat down on a wooden bench under an oak tree, and George sat down beside her. 'So,' he said quietly, 'what is it that I can help you to understand?'

'This morning, during breakfast, Lachlan received a dispatch from General Balfour, asking him to report to him as soon as possible.' A rush of colour flooded her pale cheeks. 'It seems there is an urgent need to discuss a new posting.'

'A new posting?' George pressed his lips together, restraining a smile of excitement. 'To where?'

'That's just it – Lachlan won't know until General Balfour tells him.'

George nodded, believing he understood her problem. 'That's usually the way. Such information is rarely disclosed in a dispatch. But you are troubled because ... you have no desire to leave

Scotland now?'

'No, no, that's not what troubles me. If Lachlan wished me to leave Scotland and go anywhere else in the world with him, I would go, without hesitation I would go. But not ... not ...' Elizabeth pressed a hand to her brow, covering her eyes with trembling fingers. 'But not to India ... anywhere but India.'

A difficult silence followed. George said softly, 'Because of Jane?'

'Yes...' Elizabeth admitted quietly, 'because of Jane.'

A soft rustling sound in the far bushes made George quickly glance round to catch a glimpse of Kirsteen's brown hair amongst the greenery, hiding herself as she attempted to watch and listen.

He glanced at Elizabeth and saw she had not heard the sound, but if she did become aware of Kirsteen's presence she would be mortified and would probably dismiss the maid instantly.

George felt a sudden anger and irritation, yet he contrived not to expose the girl, but this conversation was too personal, too private, to allow her to stay there.

He stood up and put his hands in his pockets and strolled slowly towards the bushes as if giving thought to the problem before answering Elizabeth.

At the bush, in the silence, he stood staring down at the hidden and crouching figure of

Kirsteen and she stared back up at him with a smiling light in her eyes, as if she had achieved some kind of victory by drawing him into her secret and over to her hiding place, and not as if she was doing anything untoward or wrong at all.

George sighed. These intrusions by the girl were becoming tiresome and unacceptable but Kirsteen was too young and too stupid to realise that.

There was a stillness about him as he continued to stand and look down at her in the silence, but the thoughts in his mind must have shown in his eyes because the expression on Kirsteen's face began to change to one of surprise and then dismay, until she began to slowly creep backwards towards the house and finally disappeared.

Only then, when he was sure she had gone, did George turn back to look at Elizabeth who was lost in her own worrying thoughts as she sat on the bench twisting her fingers together.

George had always liked Elizabeth, and now felt a very deep affection for her; but he knew he could never love Elizabeth in the way he had loved Jane, Lachlan's first wife, that beautiful and happy young girl from Antigua who had clasped him tightly in her arms as an eight-year-old boy and told him he was now *her* child, and would always be protected by *her* love, and she had even legally giving him her own surname of Jarvis to prove it to him.

In the time that followed he and Jane had gone through so much together, gone from Calicut to

Bombay together, from Bombay to China together, and every minute of every day he had simply adored her ... Jane Jarvis Macquarie ... the greatest love, and the greatest tragedy of Lachlan's Macquarie's life.

And therein lay Elizabeth's problem now, Elizabeth's dread of losing her hold on the husband she dearly loved as much as he had loved Jane.

Elizabeth Campbell had been twenty-five-years old when Lachlan and George, leaving the heartbreak of India far behind, had arrived on the Isle of Mull and met her for the first time. She had been visiting Lachlan's mother that day, and George had seen immediately that she was a young lady of the gentry, albeit the daughter of an impoverished estate run by her older brother in Airds.

In the weeks that followed, George had seen the way Elizabeth Campbell had lost her prim reserve and bubbled with laughter and life when in the company of Lachlan.

After that George saw no more of their relationship because he had been forced to go to college, so determined was Lachlan that he would receive a sound education.

And yet, two years later, George was not at all surprised when Lachlan made an unexpected visit to the college to tell him of his proposal of marriage to Elizabeth Campbell.

He and Elizabeth had found and enjoyed a

special companionship with each other, Lachlan had explained, but he could not keep Elizabeth hanging on indefinitely as a friend and nothing more. They were both still young enough for a new start, but he had been honest with Elizabeth when he had told her that his love and his heart had been given and would forever remain with Jane, but he would endeavour to be the best husband he was capable of being, which might not be a very good one. Yet Elizabeth had accepted his proposal regardless.

Cool, sensible, practical Elizabeth, she had not allowed his past to stand in the way of her happiness, and so far it had been a good match and a good marriage, marred only by the tragic loss of their beloved baby daughter.

George returned to the garden bench and sat down and looked at Elizabeth. She was thirty years old now, tall and slender with russet hair and wide blue eyes and her manner was normally full of wit, no-nonsense and absolutely charming. But look at her now ... her hands still trembling, her composure bowed low.

It distressed George to see Elizabeth so upset, and it was only recently that she had come to terms with the loss of her child – so to relieve her of this new worry would not be breaking a confidence, but simply the right thing to do.

'Elizabeth, you are worrying unnecessarily,' George said finally. 'It is all in the past now. Lachlan loved Jane then. He loves you now. That is all you need to think of.'

'I feel...' Elizabeth took a deep breath, 'that in India it would all come back to him. The life he had with her there. All the memories would come back to him, and *she* would come back to him ... not physically of course ... but in a *spiritual* way. Do you understand?'

'Yes.' George's vision was focused on some pink flowers growing at the far edge of the garden. 'But I think you are wrong in your thoughts, and worrying without cause.'

'Then help me to understand, George. You know him better than anyone, even better than I do, because you know his past, you were *there!* So why am I wrong, George? Why am I worrying without cause?'

George was still gazing at the flowers. 'Because Lachlan will never go back to India. Not even if the Army commands it. He would resign his commission if they insisted.'

'What?' A rush of colour came into her cheeks. 'How do you know this, George?'

'He told me.'

'Told you?' Elizabeth frowned in puzzlement. 'When did he tell you? You were not here this morning when the dispatch was delivered, and he had left by the time you returned.'

'He told me, some weeks before his marriage to you,' George said quietly. 'It was a decision he had already made. He knew you were his future, and India was his past. He knew the two could never be combined.'

Elizabeth sat back, as if a ton weight had been lifted off her lap, the relief making her smile happily and look lovely again. 'Oh, George, my instincts were right, I just *knew* I should speak to you first, I just *knew* you would be honest with me.'

George smiled at her, but there was sadness in his eyes and in his heart. He also would probably never go back to India, but his young mother was buried there, aged only twenty-two when she had died, and because of that India would forever be his motherland.

Chapter Three

'Was it you who put my name forward?'

'No, it was nothing to do with me. I don't enjoy such influence with the High Command.' General Balfour sulkily thrust out his bottom lip. 'I believe the culprit was Arthur Wellesley ... or as he is now called, the Duke of Wellington.'

'Wellesley?' said Lachlan, surprised. 'Wellesley recommended me for this?'

'You served with him in India, didn't you, same as me. You know that his brother has now been appointed as the Viceroy over there? Oh yes.' Balfour sulked for a second longer. 'And I believe your name was also put forward by General John Moore. You served with him in America I believe?'

Lachlan nodded. 'We were lieutenants together in Canada and New York.'

'He's just been knighted, Moore, did you know that? Anyway, between the two of them, the Duke of Wellington and General Sir John Moore, they have persuaded the Commander-in-Chief that you are the best man for the job.'

'I wish one of them had had the courtesy to consult with me first,' Lachlan said through gritted teeth. He couldn't believe it. He just couldn't believe it. 'I mean ...' he said with a puzzled frown, 'why would either of them think I would even *accept* a posting such as this?'

General Balfour looked sympathetically at the

fair tall man standing by the fireplace in absolute shock, and who wouldn't be in a state of shock in his position? This was a posting for an old sea dog, like all the other old sea dogs – not for a man still in his prime – and definitely not for a professional soldier like Lachlan Macquarie.

Balfour had known Lachlan since he was a young lieutenant just arrived in India, and he a colonel, his commanding officer. Even back then there was something about the young man that Balfour had instantly liked, and through the years and many campaigns their personal friendship had grown into something akin to uncle and nephew. Macquarie had a natural intelligence lacking in so many of the other young officers, young popinjays who had used their family's wealth and influence to buy their gold-braided uniforms and positions, unlike Macquarie who had arrived in India without a penny and had *earned* every one of his promotions.

And then there was that terrible situation with Jane ... that had crushed him, almost destroyed him, but in time the steel had returned to his resolve and he was back in the game, leading his men across the Egyptian desert to the Nile to join the rest of the British troops in a battle with the French at Alexandria.

Lachlan said irritably. 'The Duke of York – '

'Is our Commander-in-Chief,' General Balfour reminded him tersely. 'And although he is not a soldier – not in any real sense of the word – the

Duke of Wellington most definitely *is* a true soldier, as is General John Moore. And if both of these fine men have recommended you to the King, then – '

'The King!' Lachlan's shock was now turning into fury. 'But why would they do that? Without consulting with me first? And why *me* anyway? I'm not a politician, I'm simply a *soldier* for goodness sake!'

'Yes, and that's why they need someone like you now, because it is the *soldiers* over there who have been causing all the trouble.'

Balfour prised himself out of his chair and grunted. 'Let's have a drink and discuss this some more. I know by rights I should be feeling proud of you, my boy ... all these top brass recommendations ... but if you accept the post I shall be very sorry to see you go.'

After an hour of discussing it in more detail, Balfour concluded, 'Well, if nothing else, one fact still cheers me. If you *do* accept the post, you'll be back in two years. No one ever stays there for long ... it's a rotten place by all accounts. And it's a job for a strong man, a tough man. Are you that tough, Macquarie?'

Lachlan shrugged. It mattered not whether he was tough enough or not, because he had no intention of accepting the posting, he would resign his commission first.

'Well, dear boy, are you?' Balfour persisted. 'Tough enough to go to Hell and back in service of your king and country?'

Lachlan shrugged again, disinterested, and lifting his cloak to leave. 'What do you think, sir?'

'I think you're a splendid soldier and a fine man,' Balfour admitted. 'But that's all I have to say now. In the end, of course, the decision must be yours.'

*

When Lachlan returned home, Elizabeth was anxiously waiting for him at the front door.

'The dispatch – was it about a new posting? It was, wasn't it?'

'Yes.'

'To India?'

'No, but India would be like Heaven in comparison.'

'To where?' she demanded. 'In comparison to where?'

Inside the parlour Lachlan made Elizabeth sit down and then explained the contents of the dispatch to her, and the reasons behind it, in the same way Balfour had explained it to him.

'As heads of the Army and the Navy, the Duke of York and his brother the Duke of Clarence are both in a state of great alarm due to a mutiny that has taken place in the British Colony of New South Wales, deposing the Governor, William Bligh.'

'New South Wales?'

'A mutiny by the soldiers of the New South Wales Corps,' Lachlan continued.

New South Wales ... where on earth was that? Elizabeth wondered, but managed to keep silent while he went on.

'The news of the mutiny has shocked the Admiralty; this being the second that Captain Bligh has suffered. First the mutiny on *HMS Bounty*, and now another mutiny in New South Wales.

'They want Bligh replaced, and quickly.'

'By you?'

'It seems so. From what Balfour said, the Duke of York and his brother have decided that the custom of New South Wales being ruled by a succession of naval captains has become inappropriate for a place controlled solely by the military. The new Viceroy, therefore, should not be a naval commodore, but a military commander.'

Elizabeth stared at him. `And they want *you* – as Viceroy?'

'To be the new Governor-General.'

'But Lachlan ...' Elizabeth had to stand up and walk around; this was all so unexpected. 'First tell me ... *where* is this New South Wales – is it in Wales?'

'No, my love, it's somewhere on the other side of the world.'

Lachlan stood up and paused for a time to stare out of the window at the greenness of his own Scotland, still unable to believe that he had been asked to fill such a post.

He turned back to Elizabeth and gave her a wry smile as he said, 'You might have heard of the place by another name – Botany Bay.'

'Botany Bay?' No, Elizabeth had never heard of it

... and then suddenly it came to her. 'You mean, that place ... where they are sending all the criminals?'

'Yes, a penal settlement, a *convict* colony – so why would I, an active and serving *soldier,* want to go to a place like that? No more than I can understand why Arthur Wellesley and John Moore recommended me!'

'Wellesley?' Elizabeth had to sit down again. 'The Duke of Wellington recommended you?'

'Yes – sour-face himself and John Moore. So while those two are over on the continent living the life of soldiers and *fighting* Napoleon and the French – they are sending dispatches to the Duke of York saying I am the man who should be sent out to that dump-hole to oversee a crowd of stinking felons and bring a regiment of bad soldiers back into line! Look at me – do I look that old and decrepit? Do I look like my soldiering days are over?'

Elizabeth looked at her beloved husband with tears shimmering in her eyes. To her, he was the most wonderful man in the world, active and strong and full of energy ... and yes, she could fully understand his bitter feelings of betrayal against his two former friends. Why had they done it?

Lachlan's anger was consuming him to a point that he had to walk out of the room, out of the house, and then mounted his horse and rode straight back to General Balfour.

'It's because they were *asked* in dispatches from

33

the Duke of York to recommend a good man who would be up to the job,' Balfour explained. 'London doesn't care a jot about the convicts – it's the *soldiers* out there that need controlling. What London wants is a good officer who, unlike Captain Bligh, knows how to command the respect of his men, but also – a man who would also be able to command the respect of the civilian colonists as well.'

'I'll not go,' Lachlan said firmly. 'I'll resign first. My regiment is the 73rd and I'll not exchange them for a bunch of mutineers.'

'You wouldn't have to exchange them,' Balfour said, lifting a dispatch from his desk. 'This came about an hour ago, just after you had left ... It seems that London has anticipated your refusal and your reluctance to leave your own regiment ... and so they have sent this urgent dispatch informing me that they have decided to send the entire 73rd regiment out there with you.'

'What?'

'It makes sense, I suppose, now the New South Wales Corps have proved themselves to be unfit for the task. And remember, dear boy, not only would you be accompanied by your own men, you would all only be out there for about two years, quite a short posting really.'

'Oh, this is unbelievable ...' Lachlan was about to turn away and leave, and then stopped ... this latest news just beginning to sink in.

'So,' he said, turning back to General Balfour, 'if

they are preparing to send out the entire 73rd, then ...' he smiled self deprecatingly, 'well I'm just a colonel – but as commander of the regiment that means *you* are now being posted out there too.'

'I certainly am not!' Balfour exclaimed, his personal anger only now beginning to show. 'London is not going to succeed in getting *me* out to that hell-hole on the other side of nowhere – not even for two years – and I have just sent a dispatch to the Commander-in-Chief informing him of that fact. I'll take my pension instead.'

Still holding the dispatch from London, Balfour crushed the paper in his hand and then flung it into the waste-paper basket.

'And remember, Macquarie,' he said huffily, 'it's *you* they have chosen to be their new Viceroy, not me!'

Chapter Four

When Lachlan returned home Elizabeth had gone out for a walk.

'Aye an' a *long* walk it's been,' Mrs Burgess said, 'I expected her back along before this. An' young Mister George has been looking for ye. He came asking me a few times if ye were back yet.'

'Where is George?'

'He's out in the back yard, filling a bucket of water from the pump for me.'

George had his shirt sleeves rolled up and had just filled the pail when Lachlan approached him.

'Helping the servants again I see,' said Lachlan.

George shrugged a grin. 'I'm not as proud and aloof as they say I am.'

'Were you looking for me for any reason in particular?'

George straightened and began to roll down his sleeves. 'Yes, I have made a decision about my future.'

'A decision?' Lachlan felt a stab of alarm. 'Which is?'

George stood thoughtful for a moment, and then looked around him.

'Let us walk down to the field,' he suggested, 'away from the house, so our conversation is not broken by interruptions.'

They strolled down to the field in silence, and when they reached it, they rested their forearms on the gate together and Lachlan waited for George to speak.

'My life,' George said quietly, 'has got to change. I am no longer the small boy you rescued from the slave trade. I am a man now, and I want to act like a man, and live like a man.'

Lachlan frowned, perplexed.

'Your generosity, I cannot live on it anymore, take it from you anymore,' George explained. 'It's time for me to make my own way in this world, and earn my own living.'

Could this day get any worse, Lachlan wondered, and once again a sensation of impending loss swept over him. First his daughter ... and now George ... no father could love a son the way he loved George.

'Yes ... well, your education will open many doors and opportunities for you.'

George smiled in amusement. 'My education started long before I entered any classroom in London or Edinburgh. That was just a long study of books. My real education came from the life I lived in India with you and the sahibs in the British army.'

Lachlan thought back and realised that George was right. From a boy he had lived his young life amongst hardened British soldiers. Always at Lachlan's side on campaigns, he had marched with them, joked with them, and had even suffered with them all through the long march across the desert from Suez to the Nile. And when the thirst became unbearable in the cruel dry heat of that desert, George had even helped the soldiers by teaching them a trick he had learned from his Arabic mother.

Those soldiers in the 77th had loved George Jarvis, loved his laughter and good humour and repaid him by teaching him how to fight, and fight hard, in self-defence. And truth to tell, by the time they had returned from Egypt, George had changed from a boy into a hardened and strong young soldier himself.

No wonder he had found the physically lazy and soft life of college classrooms so difficult to tolerate.

'But you did well at college,' Lachlan said. 'You excelled in all your studies. And now that you are no longer forced to read books, I notice, since leaving college you spend a lot of your time doing just that – reading books.'

George laughed. 'Now I read books for pleasure not for exams. Books of my own choosing.'

'So what is this decision you have made ... about your future?'

George Jarvis did not answer for a while. Stars were appearing in the sky and the air was getting cooler.

'I want to be a soldier.'

'What?'

'A serving soldier.' George turned and looked at Lachlan, his dark eyes very serious. 'In your regiment, the 73rd.'

'The 73rd ...' Lachlan made a sound like a groan and bowed his head over his forearms on the gate. 'No, George, no ... one regiment I cannot allow you to serve in, is the 73rd.'

'Why?'

'Because, in a few weeks time, the entire 73rd regiment is being posted down to Botany Bay."

'Botany Bay?' George's interest quickened. 'Where is that?'

'Some place south of Hell.'

Chapter Five

In the end, it was not General Balfour or even the Commander-in-Chief of the Army, the Duke of York, who persuaded Lachlan Macquarie to go to New South Wales; it was the Prince of Wales.

In previous times, after his return from India and while he was working at the War Office in London as a staff officer to Lord Harrington, Lachlan had often been required to dine with the Prince of Wales in the company of his boss.

Upon receipt of his refusal of the posting, Lord Harrington sent him a dispatch a few days later.

> *The Prince of Wales remembers you well and fondly, and would consider it a personal favour if you did take the post as Governor-General of New South Wales.*
>
> *Although it has not been revealed to the country or even to Parliament, the King's health is failing badly and it is quite probable that the Prince of Wales will be taking over his duties as the King's Regent very soon.*

Lachlan looked up from the letter, realising he had no further choice in the matter. If a Regency Bill was approved by Parliament, and all royal power was vested in the Prince of Wales as Regent, then refusing his request would be tantamount to refusing the King himself.

And for a soldier ... an officer in His Majesty's Army to do that ...

But first, even before the King, Lachlan chose to give priority to consideration of the views of his family.

*

Over the previous week, Elizabeth had given long thought to the matter of New South Wales. A grim place from all accounts, and certainly not a place for a gentle-bred lady. She knew that most army wives in her position would choose to stay behind in the comfort of their own homes while their husbands were away on service.

But she also knew that if *her* husband was forced to go, and to a place so far away, no matter how awful it was she would still go with him, even to the ends of the earth, because she loved him.

*

Lachlan understood the baffled expression on George Jarvis's face.

'Why not?' George asked.

'Because if I *did* get you commissioned into the 73rd, George, all your freedom – and assistance to me – would be lost. You would be under the control of your superior officers, going out into the field, marches, parades morning and night. And it won't be anything like India or Egypt – all deployed soldiers will be there simply to *guard* the colony and the convicts.'

George at last understood. He nodded, 'Yes, yes,

I understand now.'

A silence hung in the room before George finally asked, 'So what is it you wish me to do?'

'Just to ... come with me, George. Be my personal and private aide ... Help me in this trial that I'm sure New South Wales will be. It's only for a couple of years, and you are still very young. When we return, then – '

'How soon do we go?' George asked quietly.

In blank silence Lachlan stared at him ... He knew George Jarvis had no reason that would compel him to go with him to New South Wales. Years ago, from the money left in Jane's will, a trust had been settled by her on George which he had received from the day of his twenty-first birthday. So he was financially independent now and could go wherever he pleased.

He said: 'George, it's a hellhole of convict colony ... are you sure?'

George looked at the man who had rescued him, brought him up through his childhood years and educated him, the man he would follow anywhere, because he loved him.

'Yes, my father,' George answered with certainty. 'I am sure.'

*

Two weeks later, Elizabeth and George accompanied Lachlan down to London where he was officially presented by the Duke of York to the King, who officially appointed him as Governor-

General of New South Wales, Van Diemen's Land, and all islands adjacent in the Pacific Ocean.

Unlike previous Governors of New South Wales, the new vice-regal powers that King George the Third gave "*To our trusty and well-beloved Lachlan Macquarie*," were almost those of a Monarch of the entire antipodean region.

Elizabeth could not stop herself from feeling extremely proud of the honours bestowed on her husband by the King and his sons, but Lachlan was not nearly so impressed.

'*We are shortly to be transported to a penal colony,*' he wrote to his friends in India, '*but myself and the 73rd Regiment have now become reconciled to our banishment to Botany Bay.*'

PART TWO

This fifth part of the Earth
Which would seem an after-birth
Not conceived in the Beginning,
But emerged at the first sinning,
When the ground was therefore curst;-
And hence – this barren wood!

Kangaroo

Chapter Six

As far as the white man was concerned that barren wood, founded in 1779 by Captain James Cook on the east coast of New Holland, was now a British settlement only twenty years old. Its main benefit as a newly found Crown Colony was a much-needed dumping ground for the felons who could not be contained in Britain's overflowing jails.

> Murderers, thieves, and villains,
> We'll send them all away.
> To serve out their sentence
> In the hell of Botany Bay!

No prisoners were ever landed at Botany Bay itself. In 1788, nine years after Cook's discovery, Captain Arthur Phillips arrived at Botany Bay with the first shipload of convicts, but decided that the anchorage was unsafe, finally anchoring in a beautiful harbour further up the coast, which he named Sydney.

During the twenty years since the arrival of those first prisoners, vast tracts of the barren wood had been chopped down and cleared by the energy of the convicts and the lash.

Regiments of soldiers had been dispatched there, many taking their wives and children with them. A number of free-settlers, too, had emigrated there, for wealth was always to be made in a new land, especially when the men and labour needed to make it were supplied free of wage. A man with only a few pounds might be a worthless nobody in London or Devon, but in the new colony of New South Wales he could be a land-owner, a squire, a gentleman with his own tribe of slaves!

> Southward ho!
> Away they go!
> To break the backs of convicts,
> And make their fortunes O!

The drawback to the fortune-seeking emigrant was the stigma he suffered on his return from New South Wales. The reason being that, before anything else, he had to prove his sojourn there had been *legitimate*. Even when he had proved that his time in the colony had been taken of his own free will, he was still viewed with a suspicious eye. No matter how wealthy, the returned emigrant discovered that it was a rare neighbour who could entertain his company without constantly making surreptitious checks that the contents of his pockets were safe, that his wife was safe, that his safe was safe.

Such a stigma, however, would not be suffered by Lachlan Macquarie.

*

Portsmouth harbour was bustling with activity. Two ships, the *Hindustan* and *Dromedary* had been loaded with water and supplies for the long voyage to New South Wales.

The 73rd Regiment, comprising of a thousand

soldiers and their officers, filled both ships. Well-furnished cabins had been reserved for General and Mrs Macquarie on the *Dromedary*.

Accommodation had also been found for the Macquaries' entourage of new servants, which included a cook with the appropriate name of Mrs Ovens, and a sturdy carriage-driver who stood six-feet-six-inches tall, named Joseph Bigg. The latter had been sent with personal compliments to General Macquarie from the service of Lord Harrington.

HMS Dromedary was a first rate 'Man-of-War' according to her commander, Captain Pritchard. 'Made of the best English oak, fine Welsh copper, and stout enough for anything!'

In the chill wind Elizabeth's eyes stared up at the towering masts of the ship, and then her eyes finally settled thoughtfully on the bowsprit as she wondered what lay ahead.

Seasickness.

A fierce wind astern blew them swiftly down the English Channel, the white topsails of both ships billowing and banging gustily.

Two days after leaving Portsmouth, Elizabeth was unaware that the Lizard had been passed and England left behind. She lay in her cabin sicker than she had ever been in her life, listening to the woodwork creaking all around her as the ship rolled on the swells and dipped the troughs.

She prayed for calmness, for mercy, but two more weeks of rough weather lay ahead.

Occasionally the shouts of the crew penetrated the slight lulls. '*Move it, you bugger! Where d'ye think you are? Strolling in Hyde bloody Park!*'

It was not until the weather calmed as they approached Madeira, that Elizabeth finally emerged from her cabin, pale and dazed.

On deck she saw her husband and George Jarvis, both looking as calm and relaxed as if they had spent the last three weeks on dry land.

Lachlan stared at her white face. 'My God,' he said, you look as pale as a corpse.'

'Thank you,' she said with mock sweetness. 'I *do* love your compliments.'

'*General Macquarie!*'

Lachlan turned his head to where Captain Pritchard stood by the quarterdeck rail and called down, 'A moment, sir, if you please!'

Lachlan nodded to the captain, and then assured Elizabeth. 'I'll be straight back.'

Now that she had left her cabin, Elizabeth met the other civilian passengers on board ship. Only two. A young couple, Mr and Mrs Bent, who seemed very eager to acquaint themselves with the newly-appointed Viceroy of the colony in which Ellis Bent hoped to secure a good living as an attorney or a magistrate.

In the evenings Mr and Mrs Bent often stayed up to join General and Mrs Macquarie in an after-dinner game of whist. A game which Captain Pritchard also enjoyed, except when his partner – which was usually Elizabeth – made a mistake, and he found himself forced to severely reprimand her.

'That man makes me so *cross!*' Elizabeth complained one night on the way back to their cabins. 'Who does the old sea dog think I am? One of his midshipmen!'

Smiling, Lachlan confessed that he found Captain Pritchard a likable sort of man. It was the captain of their companion ship, the *Hindustan*, who was beginning to wear his patience near the limit.

From the day they had cleared England, Captain Pascoe of the *Hindustan* had been unable to prevent himself from tearing off-course in pursuit of every strange ship he spied, convinced the ship was French, and determined to capture her and claim the prize money. All had turned out to be merely trading vessels, but thanks to Pascoe's wild pursuits they had lost many a good breeze, causing a number of delays in the process.

'Pascoe's a Merchant man,' Captain Pritchard said with a grunt when Lachlan brought up the subject, 'not Royal Navy. That's why he is mastering an Indiaman and I am commanding a King's ship.'

'Nevertheless,' Lachlan said, 'the *Hindustan* is carrying half a regiment of my soldiers. And if any of those ships *had* been French, it would have been *my* soldiers who took all of the blows and none of the profit.'

He looked through the stern window of the cabin in the direction of the trailing merchantman. 'My orders, Captain Pritchard, are to proceed to New South Wales with all possible speed.'

'As are mine,' Pritchard said, then after a thoughtful pause. 'We could, of course, leave the *Hindustan* to sail its own undisciplined course and join up with us later in New South Wales.'

Lachlan looked at him coolly. 'Would you ever, under any circumstances, desert your ship?'

Pritchard responded as if insulted. 'No, sir, never.'

'And neither will I desert my soldiers.'

Pritchard nodded. 'Aye, aye, I understand, my apologies, sir.'

Half an hour later the *Dromedary* had hove to, and sailors were dropping a boat over the side. Captain Pritchard stood by the entry port looking down as General Macquarie climbed into the longboat, but it was his own sailors that his eyes watched carefully as the boatswain shouted orders.

'Shove off! Give way all!'

Captain Pritchard watched the twin line of oars rising and falling in a strong and regular rhythm as the boat pulled swiftly across the sea towards the *Hindustan*, a quarter of a mile away.

He was still watching when the longboat and its passenger returned, the oars pulling steadily until the boatswain ordered, 'Easy all!' and the two lines of dripping oars rose up in the air like the two wings of an albatross; and the bowman swiftly hooked the boat on to the chains of the ship.

Captain Pritchard called down his approval to

the boatswain, his voice deliberately loud. 'Expertly done, Mr Hawkins. Expertly done!'

It was praise meant for all the boat's crew, but it had to be addressed to their petty officer, Mr Hawkins, who was making sure that General Macquarie did not slip between boat and ship as he climbed up the side steps, acknowledged the praise with a smile but without lifting his eyes. 'Thank you, Captain.'

Pritchard greeted Macquarie as he stepped back on board. 'You spoke to Pascoe?'

Lachlan nodded. 'I spoke to Pascoe.'

And as Macquarie walked away, Pritchard had a feeling that that, too, had been expertly done.

*

The journey went on, over miles and miles of empty sea with never a view of land. Elizabeth and Mrs Bent spent their days in the manner of most seafaring passengers on their first long voyage: when the weather was hot and becalmed, with no wind to aid their progress, they got in a bad mood and blamed the captain, attributing to him at least twenty faults which he probably did not possess.

When a fair breeze finally arrived, permitting the ship to sail speedily and steadily, their good humour was instantly restored, and the captain forgiven.

Captain Pritchard, meanwhile, was becoming very impressed with the care and attention General Macquarie constantly gave to his troops. Not the smallest detail relating to their comfort and health was overlooked.

Macquarie personally ensured that all provisions served to the men were of the best quality and well cooked. Each day he inspected those parts of the ship that housed his troops, insisting their decks be kept as clean as possible, and stressed the importance of all hammocks being kept dry.

'In warm weather,' Captain Pritchard heard Macquarie instructing his officers, 'all hatchways must remain open so as much air as possible can be allowed inside.'

Oh no, Captain Pritchard thought to himself with certainty, no soldier on the *Dromedary* would be allowed to die of pneumonia or pleurotic fever or catch even the smallest infection, not if their commanding officer could prevent it.

And now, of the three hundred and seventy soldiers aboard the *Dromedary* all remained very healthy.

Not so on the *Hindustan*.

All Lachlan's fears came to fruition when Captain Pascoe sent a cutter to the *Dromedary* to inform General Macquarie that there was a severe outbreak of dysentery on board his ship, and the sick list of soldiers was increasing by the day. Some were now so ill they needed the care of a hospital.

Nor could Captain Pascoe hope for a favourable change in the condition of the soldiers, having nothing but salt provisions, and his supply of water had run so short he had insufficient to carry them to the Cape of Good Hope.

Lachlan said to Captain Pritchard. 'Now you see why it was so important that the two ships should never part company! The *Hindustan* needs vegetables and water and we can supply them immediately.'

'That would reduce our own supplies drastically.'

'Our own supplies can be supplemented at the nearest port,' Lachlan replied impatiently. 'And many of those men on the *Hindustan* are so ill they will die if they don't receive water and medical help soon. So tell me – which is our nearest port?'

'The nearest port is miles off our charted course.' Captain Pritchard was already peering at the chart on his desk, finally stabbing it with his finger. 'Rio de Janeiro ... miles off in the opposite direction. We would lose a lot of time.'

'Or we could save that time and lose a lot of decent young men instead. Which would you prefer?'

Pritchard looked up, alerted by the undertone of anger in Macquarie's words.

'Well,' he said, turning his gaze back to the map, 'I would prefer to carry on to the Cape ... but, in view of the sick men, I suppose I have no choice but to veer way off course and head southwest to Rio.'

*

The spectacular beauty and grandeur of the harbour of Rio de Janeiro on a fine clear evening was enough in itself, without the extra splendour of the red sun slowly setting behind the Sugar Loaf.

Elizabeth stood at the ship's rail beside Lachlan and stared at the scene in awe. A good wind had carried them in, and the town of St Sebastian could clearly be seen. Church spires pierced the skyline and perched on her hills the town of St Sebastian was surrounded on all sides by the magnificent houses of noblemen. Here, at last, was the architectural *art* of the Portuguese.

If there's one thing the Doms do well,' Lachlan said, 'it's building beautiful houses.'

'*Let go!*' a voice yelled, followed by a thundering crash as the ship's anchor plunged into the water.

Now steady in her anchorage, Lachlan left the *Dromedary* to be rowed across in a gig to the *Fondroyant*, a Portuguese flagship of 80 guns.

As soon as Admiral de Courcy heard about the sick soldiers on the *Hindustan,* all were lifted off the ship and placed in the hospital at St Sebastian. The hospital had once been a nobleman's house, the rooms spacious and airy.

Every day Lachlan visited the soldiers in the hospital. All were comfortable, all spoke favourably of their treatment by the Portuguese, but none were well enough to return to ship.

'Another week,' Lachlan told them. 'That is all the time we can spare you. After that, we must continue our journey to New South Wales.'

*

New South Wales, and the mutiny that had taken

place there, was a subject that occupied most of Lachlan's thoughts in the following days. The only information he possessed regarding the state of the colony was the same as that known in London. He had not expected to discover any further information until reaching the Cape of Good Hope. And even there, he thought the prospect of any news was doubtful.

But now a trading vessel from Sydney, en route to England, had docked at Rio de Janeiro. It carried two passengers, a Mr Jameson and a Mr Harris.

Admiral de Courcy provided a small boat and sent both men over to the *Dromedary* to report to General Macquarie.

Mr Harris, a short, pompous-mannered man, talked the most, eager to impress, but it was Mr Jameson who gave all the information.

Governor Bligh, who was supposed to be under military house arrest, had managed to escape and board his own ship, the *Porpoise*, and set sail for England.

Two of the leaders of the rebellion, Major Johnston and John McArthur, had also sailed for England, determined to lay their version of the mutiny alongside those of Captain Bligh.

Jameson then told Lachlan something else about New South Wales – something very important. The officers who had instigated the mutiny against Governor Bligh had proved to possess little experience of organising a settlement on any practical or economic level. The government storehouses were almost empty, all forms of price restraint had collapsed, and a flood from the Blue Mountains had destroyed the crops.

A new Governor and a new regiment might restore control, but what good was that when the colony faced the possibility of starvation? Many of the convicts were indeed starving. And since the mutiny, England had sent no money to support the Government of New South Wales.

'The reason for that, Mr Jameson, is because there is no official Government in New South Wales, only a band of mutineers.'

'Who have proved to be very bad managers,' Jameson said. 'The soldiers are almost in as bad a state as the convicts. With no Government money, no cloth could be bought to replace old uniforms. And the shoes that are usually handed out from the Government store to the soldiers and convicts are long gone now. All used up and no money to buy more. It's a disgraceful sight, sir, uniforms in tatters and shoes held together with string.'

Lachlan sat back in utter dismay. How could soldiers in ragged uniforms ever command authority or respect!

He looked intently at Jameson. 'And you, sir? Why are *you* leaving New South Wales?'

'Me?' Jameson seemed taken aback at the question. 'Why, I'm doing what most free settlers eventually do. I'm returning home – back to a civilised country where a gentleman doesn't have to breathe the same air as felons. Five long years I've been in that country of thieves, and that's enough.'

After a pause, Jameson went on, 'Five years is longer than any Governor has stayed. Bligh lasted less than two. Even Governor King –'

'Thank you, Mr Jameson,' Lachlan said, his tone making it clear that the subject of past governors was now closed.

*

It was almost evening the following day when Jameson's name was mentioned again, this time by George Jarvis, who had been ashore to deliver a letter from Lachlan to Sir James Gamlin, the British Consul.

Lachlan was standing on deck watching the trading vessel with its two passengers from Sydney sailing smoothly out of the harbour of Rio de Janeiro, bound for England.

'Mr Jameson,' said George, handing Lachlan a letter. 'Is he the one who told you about the starving convicts and soldiers in bad shoes?'

Lachlan opened Sir James's letter of reply. 'Yes, Mr Jameson.'

'Yes, it was him I saw.' George said. 'The one who left your cabin as I entered, the one who said it was his pleasure as a *gentleman* to be of help to you.'

'George, speak sense.'

'Him – Mr Jameson,' George explained. 'I saw

him this morning in the market at St Sebastian. He was selling crate-loads of merchandise to the traders. "From New South Wales," he told them. The money they paid him was very good.'

'Selling?' Lachlan looked at him curiously. 'What was he selling?'

'Shoes,' George answered. 'Two crate-loads of men's new shoes.'

Lachlan stood in silence, his eyes distant on the departing trading vessel, cruising away with all sails full, bound for England, and carrying a handsome profit made by two gentleman from New South Wales.

George continued: 'I don't know if it was Mr Harris, but a second man later joined Jameson. A small man who acted like a nabob, and he too began selling – boxes of men's "colonial-made boots and stockings – from New South Wales".'

Lachlan remained silent. He turned slowly and gazed over the decks of the *Dromedary*. Most of his own soldiers were on leave ashore, but the ship's sailors were to be seen everywhere aboard. He looked up, head back, and watched a figure skimming fearlessly up the mainmast, probably to carry out some small repair.

Finally, he looked aft at the blue and white uniforms of the officers on the poop deck, then said, 'See those officers there, George, they also claim to be gentlemen. They enter the Navy as gentlemen and they live and mess as gentlemen. Their duties and responsibilities are far different to the common seaman. And they have a saying ... "We officers are gentleman, we never pull a rope."'

He looked at George. 'So it's odd, isn't it, that two men who loudly profess to be *gentlemen* should spend their morning selling shoes in the St Sebastian market. Crates of shoes and boots that must have come from the Government stores in Sydney, intended for provision to soldiers.'

'So, you are saying – '

'I am *thinking*, George, that the line in New South Wales might not be so clearly drawn. If our two visitors are an example, I may find it hard to know where a felon ends and a gentleman begins.'

*

Captain Pritchard had been unwell for days. At dinner the following evening he appeared unable to eat.

'Ladies and gentlemen,' he said finally, 'if you will excuse me...'

Lachlan rose from his seat. 'Do you need a doctor?'

Pritchard shook his head. He had never trusted doctors, and wasn't about to start now. 'Useless drunkards most of 'em!'

'Surely someone should escort you to your cabin,' Elizabeth said, but all offers of help were brushed aside.

'When I am unwell,' the captain said irritably, 'I prefer to be left entirely to myself.'

He returned to his cabin and his bed, leaving his

passengers very uneasy about his condition. As each hour passed the change in his personality was a revelation. From a solid, calm and pleasant man in health, Captain Pritchard metamorphosed into a cantankerous old goat when sick.

Having claimed a preference to be left alone, he kept two or three servants busily employed answering his calls hour after hour, attempting to attend to his needs, only to be roared at again and again that he did *'not like to be touched!'*

At midnight his servants were rescued from their exhausted confusion by the arrival of General Macquarie.

'I'm sorry to disturb you, Captain,' Lachlan said with a quiet gentleness. 'I just came to find out, at which hour of the night, do you intend to allow the rest of us to sleep?'

'It's well for you that you *can* sleep!' Pritchard roared. 'Your cabins are bigger and more comfortable than mine!'

Lachlan glanced around the captain's sleeping cabin which was indeed very confined, and must be even moreso when the servants were in attendance.

'It's the blasted guns!' Pritchard roared. 'I told you, sir, this ship is a man-of-war. And because of that I must share my sleeping compartment with an eight-pounder cannon!'

He grunted sourly. 'The reason being, of course, that some guns had to be removed and found storage space in order to provide spacious and comfortable accommodation for yourself and Mrs Macquarie.'

'In that case,' Lachlan said, 'allow me to offer you the comfort of my own cabin, at least while you are ill.'

'Oh that *would* be a blessing!' Pritchard cried. 'More space for my servants and more air for me.' He wiped at the sweat on his face. 'But where will *you* sleep?'

'With my wife.'

Lachlan studied the shocked expression on the captain's face. 'It's not unusual, you know, for a man to sleep with his wife.'

'It's something I have never done at sea,' Pritchard replied sourly; and as his wife always remained at their home in Portsmouth, Lachlan fully understood why.

Lachlan turned to George Jarvis who was standing by the door. 'The captain is removing temporarily to my cabin, George. Make the arrangements with his servants, will you. And send for his first lieutenant.'

I can't walk,' Pritchard said sullenly. 'Legs are gone. Ceased up without warning. Rheumatism is as big a curse to a seaman's legs as rot is to a ship's hull.'

Nor would he allow any of his own men to carry him, not even his servants. 'I don't like them to *touch* me! Makes them familiar, lessens their respect! In his own ship a captain must always be king! At least to his crew!'

'Some soldiers, then?' Lachlan suggested, inwardly admiring his own patience.

'Not soldiers! Too clumsy. I don't want to be trundled about like a cannon.'

Captain Pritchard cocked an eye. 'What about your own servants, General? Are any strong enough to haul me forward without damaging my hull?'

'Very well,' Lachlan agreed patiently, 'I'll send for some of own my servants.' He turned to George. 'See if Joseph Bigg is awake, and if not wake him and – '

'What about *him*?' Pritchard interrupted curiously, pointing a finger at George. 'He don't look like no ruffian but he's still a servant isn't he?'

George offered Lachlan a careless smile, but Lachlan's tone to Pritchard was cold. 'No, sir, he is not a servant. He is a member of my family.'

'What?' Captain Pritchard looked astounded. 'But he's a brownie! An Arab of some sort – '

'Who may as well help you to get some sleep,' George concluded, giving Lachlan a significant look conveying his lack of offence at the captain's understandable ignorance. 'Will you let me help you, sir?'

'There, see, I knew you were a good `un,' said Captain Pritchard sitting up in his bed, 'as refined as any white man. Now *you* take me by my top half, and leave my feet to the other servants.'

Inside her cabin Elizabeth lay in her berth, leaning up on one elbow, her expression disbelieving as George Jarvis and Joseph Bigg carried the captain through the mess-cabin to his new sleeping quarters, still shouting as many orders as he had breath to voice.

'Avast! Avast! *Avast!*'

'Bloody 'ell, what does that mean?' she heard Joseph Bigg exclaim frustratedly.

'Stop,' she heard George reply. 'Avast is naval language for stop, Joseph.'

'Look, stop wittering and *avast* heaving I say!' Pritchard roared. 'Have a care for my larboard side! Now hoist together. Hold on ... hold on – you *must* heave me in at the larboard side! Now hoist! Now slew me round to starboard! Steady... *steady* ...'

Some minutes later, Lachlan wearily stepped through the adjoining door and looked bleakly at Elizabeth, the captain's voice behind him, still haranguing George Jarvis and Joseph Bigg. Nothing anyone did or said could please him.

Lachlan pulled the door firmly shut behind him. 'At least he is now bedded.'

'Is he to remain here with us throughout his illness?'

'I'm afraid so.'

She buried her face into the pillow as the captain's voice roared on.

Lachlan untied his neckcloth and sat down on the berth beside her. 'This,' he said tiredly, 'has been a very bad night.'

She sat up and put her lips to his shoulder. 'My

poor darling,' she murmured.

He glanced at her. As usual she had taken down her bronze hair and brushed it, long and loose, over the shoulders of her white nightgown. She did not look like the Elizabeth of the day. In the day, in the eyes of all watchers, she was always the strait-laced and sensible Elizabeth. But once in the privacy of their rooms, that side of her known only to him unfolded itself.

In the adjoining cabin the uproar continued, Pritchard shouting to Joseph Bigg to fetch his own servants, then roaring at George to *'Come back here Jarvis! I told you, I must NOT be left alone!'*

Lachlan sighed. 'Everyone else, perhaps, but his temper will not faze George.'

Both listened as the captain's voice barked on through the thin wood-panel of wall that divided them.

'No, Jarvis, I don't *want* any medicine! Put it down! And to hell with your cursed calmness! I've been watching you for weeks, my lad! You have the manner of someone above your true station! Dressed like a gentleman you may be, but you're nothing more than a brown-skinned galley slave!'

'We are all mere puppets of our heavenly master.' George's voice sounded amused.

'Damnation, Jarvis! Are you *always* so calm? Do you *never* get vexed or befuddled?'

'What we shall be is written, and we are so.'

'Well, drot! Is that what your great prophet Mohammed says, eh?'

'No, Captain, those are the words of a Persian Poet who lived six hundred years ago. Omar Khayaam.'

'There you go again! As cool as a whore's heart! I don't know why or how Macquarie tolerates you.'

'In life as on ship,' George's voice sounded resigned, 'we must tolerate those we must tolerate.'

Lachlan frowned at Elizabeth. 'I don't merely tolerate him.'

'George knows that.' She let out a gentle breath and lay back on the pillows. 'But tonight we are *all* tolerating the captain.'

The hurricane lamp on the wall threw its usual shadows around the room, moving slightly from side to side with the ship's gentle motion. A black streak of shadow had fallen on her bronze hair, reminding him of the skin of an Indian tiger cub.

He bent down and kissed her.

*

They awoke in the morning to the blissful sound of silence.

'I suppose,' Lachlan said as he dressed, 'I should go in and enquire of our neighbour.'

'If you must.' Elizabeth looked at him tiredly. 'But if he starts his shouting again I will go in and box his ears, I will.'

Lachlan gently tapped on the adjoining door, and then gingerly opened it, but the bird had flown. The cabin was empty.

Up on deck, the ship's first lieutenant wearily explained what had happened. 'As soon as your people had left him, General, he sent for us and insisted upon being transported back to his own cabin.'

Lachlan couldn't believe it. 'So all that moving him in the night was for nothing?'

'I'm afraid so, sir.'

'Is his condition any better?'

'His condition is the same, sir, but his temper is much worse.'

Lachlan blinked. 'Worse? Is that possible?'

The lieutenant sighed apologetically. 'I'm sorry, General Macquarie, but the captain is always unwell when we spend too long in an unscheduled port. He rarely enjoys the sight of land, except when it's Portsmouth. Like the rest of us, his world is the open sea.'

'Will his health recover once we set sail again?'

'Oh, certainly.'

And so it proved, three days later, when the almost-recovered soldiers had been evacuated from the hospital in St Sebastian and returned to their ship.

As soon as he heard they were ready to sail, Captain Pritchard rushed directly to the quarterdeck where he dressed himself while giving orders to his first-lieutenant, which were then repeated over the ship through the lieutenant's trumpet.

'Stand by on the capstan!'

Captain Pritchard pulled on his seagoing coat.

'Hands aloft! Loose Tops'ils!'

Seeing General and Mrs Macquarie watching him, Captain Pritchard touched his hat cheerfully to them, his personality transformed.

'*Man the braces!*'

Elizabeth was smiling with relief. 'There appears to be nothing wrong with his legs or his health now!'

George Jarvis frowned. 'No, not his physical health, but I am still not sure about his *mind*. There is a word for it, when a man has two personalities ...'

'Mad!' Elizabeth decided, linking her arm in George's and giving him a loving squeeze.

The three of them stood together at the rail, looking back at Rio de Janeiro as the ship swung away from her. The Sugar Loaf began to dwindle into a smudge and before them lay miles upon miles of open sea.

*

Upon reaching Cape Town, Lachlan left Elizabeth in the entertaining care of the British Consul and his wife, allowing himself and George Jarvis no time to spare on socialising. It took four days of hard work to load a ship with fresh water and supplies, but that was Captain Pritchard's concern. Lachlan was more preoccupied with obtaining supplies for New South Wales.

'If the Government storehouses in Sydney are empty,' he said to George, 'then they must be refilled, and as soon as possible.'

He hired a large trading vessel and had it loaded with six thousand pounds of flour, one hundred tons of grain, and all other essential supplies that the Cape could provide.

His final purchase – which he entrusted to George, Jarvis, aided by six soldiers, was to purchase every pair of men's regular shoes in every size available, eventually filling six crates; followed by the purchase of ten bales of red broadcloth and ten bales of white linen.

Captain John Antill, Lachlan's military aide, was surprised by this final purchase.

'The regiment is well kitted-out, sir, and we have our own supplies of shoes and broadcloth on board.'

Lachlan nodded, '*We* may be well supplied, Captain, but the soldiers of the New South Wales Corps are going to be sent back home in disgrace because of the mutinous behaviour of their senior officers, so the least I can do for them is to make sure they arrive back in England looking as good as when they left it, as well-dressed soldiers of His Majesty's 46th Regiment.'

When Captain Antill made no reply, Lachlan looked at him questioningly. 'Would *you* wish to arrive back in England barefoot and in rags, Captain? After three years of service on the other side of the world, would *you* wish your family and neighbours to see you in such a state?'

Captain Antill's young face flushed crimson at the very thought of such an embarrassment. 'No, sir.'

'Nor I, nor any one of my soldiers in the 73rd,' Lachlan replied tersely.

Antill flushed again. 'My apologies, sir.'

A short time later Lachlan returned to the waterfront where the crates were still being hauled aboard the trading vessel with the help of ropes.

As soon as she was fully loaded and ready, the ship's captain was instructed to weigh anchor and set sail with all possible speed for New South Wales.

Three days later, the *Dromedary* and the *Hindostan,* carrying the 73rd Regiment, set their sails and left the port of Cape Town heading towards the same destination of New South Wales.

Chapter Seven

Week after week they saw nothing but an immense empty ocean without even a bird to keep them company, without even a sight of another ship, until it seemed as if the *Dromedary* and the *Hindustan* had the whole world to themselves, a world without other humans, a watery world without end.

Elizabeth's mood had completely changed. The *Dromedary* no longer felt like a familiar home to her now, but a prison.

The mornings which she usually spent in her cabin reading books and writing letters in a social manner had now lost all their joy. In Cape Town, Lachlan had bought her a quill-pen with a new-fashioned steel nib, and she used it now lethargically:

We are all very tired of living at sea. The motion of the ship has given me a confounded fuzz in my head, which makes me feel very much out of sorts; I can't enjoy anything, I feel very cross –

Elizabeth found Lachlan at the desk in his cabin, frowning as he carefully studied his papers on New South Wales, lists upon lists of convicted prisoners and the reason for their transportation.

'Lachlan, we have been at sea for seven months now.'

'So?' he answered, not taking his eyes from the papers.

'Do you think,' she asked him seriously, 'that Captain Pritchard has got his charts wrong and we are not only lost, but lost within that triangle from which ships never emerge?'

He looked up at her vaguely. 'What triangle?'

'I've heard the seamen speak of it,' she told him gravely. 'A lost triangle of ocean that is walled by thick mists of fog, and any ship that loses its way and mistakenly slips through the fog into the triangle never finds it way out again, never. "*The Sailors Eternity*" they call it.'

He laid down his papers and looked at her, and now that she had achieved his full attention she voiced her worst suspicion of all.

'Do you remember that blanket of fog we encountered a few weeks ago? It lasted all through the night, a thick cloud of fog, but in the morning it had cleared. And since then we've not seen even a bird...'

'Elizabeth, don't be silly.'

'What!'

Lachlan spoke quietly. 'Elizabeth, are you still suffering from confusion in your head?'

'No – and what has my head got to do with it?'

'I know that we have been at sea a long time,' he replied, 'and it can lead to disorientation. But I assure you, we are not lost in any mythical "Sailors Eternity," we are right on course, heading for the Bass Strait.'

She turned and left him without a word, feeling very cross at his accusation that she was being silly. She went on deck and met Mrs Ovens who was shaking her head slowly.

'It's all too silent for me,' said Mrs Ovens fearfully. 'Oh, Mrs Macquarie, m'dear, I fear we may be lost and no one is telling us.'

'Nonsense!' said Elizabeth, tapping the cook's plump hand reprovingly as she would to a silly child. 'I assure you, Mrs Ovens, we are not lost at all, but right on course, heading for the Bass Strait.'

'And where might that be?'

Elizabeth drew in a deep breath of sea air. 'Oh, not very far from our destination of New Holland.'

Mrs Ovens looked pleased, although – as she said to Joseph Bigg later – she was surprised when Mrs Macquarie had said that, about New Holland – because she had always understood they were going to New South Wales.

Joseph Bigg looked down his nose at the fat little cook and said condescendingly, 'It's in New 'Olland, is New Souf Wales.'

'Is it? Well no one told *me* that!'

'Well now *I'm* telling you, ain't I? New Souf Wales is in the continent of New 'Olland. Right slap bang in the middle of it!'

'Then how comes they say we'll be there as soon as the ship docks? A ship can't dock in the middle of a continent. Even I knows that.'

Joseph Bigg disregarded her question entirely

and returned his eyes to the open sea.

*

In his cabin, Lachlan was still engrossed in his papers on New South Wales, and still frowning. While studying the records of his future charges, he had been utterly astonished at the number of crimes which had been marked down by the British magistrates as indicating "inherent evil" in the culprits, and which had resulted in transportation to the other side of the world.

A young girl of ten had filched a pie; another had stolen a lady's lace handkerchief; another a pair of stockings; another a strip of lace from her mistress's sewing-box.

Boys who had stolen carp out of someone else's pond or snatched fish out of private rivers; cooking a rabbit in the open after sundown. The list of young men and women who had married secretly, without the permission of their masters, was endless, and the sentence unduly severe – fourteen years in Botany Bay.

'Look,' he said to Elizabeth later, 'look at these lists of hardened and vicious criminals! Some are no more than children! Look at this one – a young girl of twelve, of a good family, who foolishly borrowed and rode a neighbour's pony in a schoolgirl frolic – sentenced to seven years in Botany Bay! That neighbour must have been the Devil himself.'

Elizabeth was also appalled as she read through

the lists. There were vicious criminals there to be sure, but most were young adults who had committed various offences, none of any great calamity, but amongst them were scores upon scores of children whose crime would be considered as little more than a misdemeanour by any rational person.

'And look here,' said Lachlan. 'An English soldier wounded on the battlefields of Europe and left crippled in one leg – seven years in Botany Bay for stealing a broom! A *broom*, for God's sake! He probably wanted to use it as a crutch.'

He returned to the records and read on through the lists of hardened criminals awaiting the iron hand of his rule.

In the past year alone, five girls of eleven years had been transported; seven girls of twelve years; thirty-two of fourteen years; sixty-five of fifteen years. The numbers for boys were even higher. All filchers of some little thing or another, and all sentenced to seven years in Botany Bay. He shook his head slowly. How on earth was he going to deal with such dangerous criminals?

They were both still studying the lists when George Jarvis called to them excitedly to come up on deck—a seal had surfaced near the ship.

'A seal?' Lachlan smiled at Elizabeth. 'The appearance of a seal usually means that land is not too far away.'

Later they saw a number of whales. One came quite close to the ship, a big playful old thing that bobbled alongside, spurting water at them.

They were in the Bass Strait. Every day their eyes were distanced on the far horizon, until they finally glimpsed land, then watched it draw closer and closer until the white cliffs of New South Wales stood outlined under a vivid blue sky.

*

Eight months after leaving England, the *Dromedary* and *Hindustan* lay at anchor in Sydney harbour. The vessel that Lachlan had hired and filled with provisions at the Cape of Good Hope had arrived only two days before them, and now had unloaded all her cargo to the delight of the hungry population of Sydney.

The harbour was already filling with people hoping to catch an early glimpse of the new Governor, but the *Dromedary* was standing too far out for them to see anything more than a number of shadowy figures scuttling up and down the masts as she dropped all her canvas.

On their last night on board ship, a double ration of grog was served to both soldiers and sailors, speeches of gratitude were made to the captain and crew, and later music and singing could be heard drifting over the water.

In the darkness Lachlan, Elizabeth and George stood on deck and looked across the glistening sheet of black water at the lights of Sydney twinkling from the various levels of the town.

'It looks so small,' George said, and Lachlan

agreed. 'As small as the harbour of Tobermory ... maybe it will look different in daylight.'

Elizabeth said nothing as she stared at the distant lights, because for the first time she felt a desperate wave of homesickness, realising that she was now totally separated from her own country by two oceans and twelve thousand miles, and was now even on a different half of the globe.

She could not help wondering, with some apprehension, what lay ahead of them.

Chapter Eight

The morning sun blazed across Sydney harbour, the sky clear and blue, the air hot and humid, for although it was deep winter in England, it was the beginning of summer in the new world.

A fleet of boats had been rowing back and forth from the ships for almost an hour, bringing ashore the soldiers of the 73rd Regiment: but as soon as Lachlan Macquarie stepped onto the wharf, dressed in scarlet regimentals and surrounded by his officers, the powder of fifteen cannons roared out salutes of welcome.

Nearly every inhabitant of the settlement, free settlers, emancipists, and a large number of convict-servants had come out eagerly to see the man who was to be their new ruler.

This was the man who had been decent enough, and intelligent and humane enough, to give consideration to their plight and take action to remedy their hunger as soon as he had heard about it, even before he had arrived here in the colony.

They saw he was tall, fair and trim with a fine military carriage, and not short and round-shouldered like that old sea dog Captain Bligh. They also liked the fact that he had also brought with him a ship loaded with more desperately needed supplies – most Governors usually only brought trouble.

At the Pier, Colonel Paterson and Lieutenant-

Colonel Foveaux of the New South Wales Corp were waiting with prominent 'Gentlemen of the Settlement.' But it was the soldiers of General Macquarie's own 73rd Regiment who formed a guard, under arms, for his passage along the short route up to Government House.

The gentleman of the settlement and their wives bowed deferentially to the new Viceroy: these were the self-styled aristocracy of the colony, known as 'Exclusives,' because of their creed of not mixing with emancipists or any person who had once been a convict.

A group of young female convict-servants had managed to get a place near the edge of the crowd. Some climbed up into the trees for a better view. These girls needed no chains, no prison doors. Their walls were the ocean and the impenetrable wild bush. They had very soon learned that there was no escape from Botany Bay.

*

Government House, naturally enough, was the most lavish house in the colony. A white mansion, with the Union Jack fluttering above the entrance, and standing within four acres of gardens and lawns which sloped down to the Governor's private wharf and a crescent of sandy beach.

Elizabeth stood in the drawing room staring at one of the full-length windows that looked onto the garden. '*My God!*' she gasped in shock. '*Oh my God!*'

Her cry brought Lachlan in from the reception hall where he had been standing talking with his officers. 'Elizabeth?'

Elizabeth pointed to the full-length window.

A young Aboriginal boy of about twelve years was standing there, peering in – black-skinned and as naked as the day he was born.

As soon as he saw Lachlan in his red-coated uniform, the Aboriginal boy waved excitedly, shouting through the glass, '*Halloo new Gubnor! Halloo Gubnor's lady! Halloo! Halloo!*'

Lachlan grinned, the sight was no different to those he had often seen in India. 'He's just being friendly.'

Elizabeth turned abruptly and walked hurriedly towards the door. 'I think I will go and meet the kitchen staff now rather than later.'

Red-faced she pushed her way through the crowd of officers in the hall and, after a polite enquiry to a maid, headed towards the kitchens.

*

The Governor's household consisted of over ninety servants, male and female. There were two kitchen buildings: the smallest kitchen being for the preparation of meals for the Governor's personal household, which would now be presided over by Mrs Ovens. And a second, vastly larger kitchen, for the preparation of food for the staff, presided over by Mrs Kelly.

Elizabeth stood in the massive staff-kitchen

looking round at the battalion of young maids who were scrubbing and cleaning.

She turned to Mrs Kelly who was robustly plump, as most cooks usually are, and was about to make a polite inquiry about the ages of the girls, but the stout woman shook her head vigorously and sought to pre-empt Elizabeth's question.

'There's no thieves in here, m'lady,' said Mrs Kelly in a rich Irish lilt. 'I won't have thieves in my kitchen. Not for a minute I won't! No, nearly all these lasses ye see here are Irish lasses, m'lady, out in Botany for being rebels.'

Rebels?' Elizabeth cast a startled glance at the girls.

'Oh then, it's not worried ye need be, m'lady,' Mrs Kelly quickly assured her, 'because they're all innocent. That they are! Innocent victims of informers who were paid for as many as they could name and frame. And that's why Irish lasses like these are known in Botany as *pretty pictures* – because of them being framed.'

Elizabeth looked with dubious cynicism at the cook. 'Surely that's not the truth?'

'It is, God knows.' Mrs Kelly heaved a wavering sigh that wafted over the entire kitchen, and Elizabeth had never realised so much pathos could be expressed in one sigh.

'God knows,' said the cook, 'that all these poor unfortunate girls are victims of injustice. And as for my English girls...'

Mrs Kelly rapidly pointed here and there,

singling out the English girls.

'Why, most are merely imps who got up to some little prank and no more. Now, young Gracie there ...' She pointed to a small fair-haired girl of very delicate looks. 'Gracie is my own little cockney sparrow. Like a daughter to me is Gracie. And hers is a very sad story.'

Gracie, at the sink, turned and gave the Governor's lady a shy smile, then dropped a little curtsy, as she had been instructed to do.

Elizabeth smiled back, which seemed to surprise the girl, sending a bright blushing colour into her face, which made her look extremely sweet.

'Gracie,' said Mrs Kelly, 'was only eleven when she left the workhouse in Billingsgate, but within hours she was taken advantage of by two men – two brutes who left her raped and bruised and weeping. They was seen and caught though, and hauled in by the constables and charged. But what did the two maulers say to the judge? They swore on the Bible that Gracie was a prostitute! And she only a child of eleven! And what's more – Gracie is partly dumb and couldn't even speak in defence of herself, on account of her taking so long to get a sentence out. But the judge was in a hurry, so what did he do to our poor little stuttering Gracie? He sent her out to Botany for seven years without giving her a hearing. Isn't that terrible? Isn't that a crime?'

Mrs Kelly looked at Elizabeth as if expecting at least a nod, but Elizabeth knew it would be imprudent to make a comment.

Instead she said curiously, 'And what about you, Mrs Kelly? Are you a rebel too? May one ask?'

Mrs Kelly huffed and puffed as if unprepared for the question. She pushed a strand of hair away from her brow with a distracted air, and then, after another heavy sigh, looked demurely at Elizabeth. 'It was never proved, m'lady, so I am innocent too.'

'Of what?'

The cook glanced round the kitchen at the girls and then lowered her voice into a confessional whisper. 'I was charged, m'lady, with a crime of passion against my unfaithful lover.'

'Indeed?' Elizabeth looked at the big buxom woman and decided not to probe further. 'And how long, Mrs Kelly, have you been here?'

'In Botany? Eighteen years, m'lady. But I earned my Pardon eleven years ago. So I'm as free to leave the colony as you are.'

'And yet you choose not to go back to Ireland?'

'And leave my poor chicks with no mother to care for them?' Mrs Kelly shook her head. 'What would my Gracie do without me for a start? No, it's here I'm needed badly. And sure, what would there be for me back in Ireland once it was learned I was in Botany Bay? I'd not get a job in a lovely kitchen like this.'

Mrs Kelly straightened her apron. 'No, m'lady, thank you for asking, but I'm happy where I am. And I hope my cooking and service will be as satisfactory to yourself and His Excellency the new

Governor as it was to Governor Bligh and Governor King.'

'I'm sure it will,' Elizabeth smiled.

Another of Mrs Kelly's sighs wafted over the kitchen, and again Elizabeth caught Gracie smiling sweetly at her as she turned to leave.

'There now, me darlings,' Mrs Kelly cried robustly before Elizabeth was even out the door, 'I think we'll find life a whole lot more respectable now there is a woman in charge of Government House. That we will! And remember what I told yiz – yiz'll not go wrong in this life if you have nothing to do with men – wicked, *wicked* men!'

*

Although Government House was indeed the grandest residence in all of Sydney, George Jarvis gave his mind no time to be impressed by its spacious rooms and elegant furnishings, because in his mind he could still remember the cool shaded rooms of a palace in Surat, with gold goblets and ruby and sapphire-encrusted fruit trays, all left lying about so carelessly in the chamber of rooms where he and his mother had lived.

But he *was* impressed, truly impressed, by the sight before his eyes now.

George's living quarters in Government House were next to Lachlan and Elizabeth's on the upper floor of the house; a small sitting-room and a larger bedroom with a closet for washing and dressing, all nice enough, but it was the view from the windows that impressed and entranced him.

From the window he stood and gazed on what Captain Pritchard had described as the most beautiful harbour in the world, *"even more beautiful than the harbour at Rio,"* and Sydney Harbour truly was beautiful with its sandy beaches and inlets of the bluest water shimmering under the golden sun.

Long ago it seemed now, in Cochin, as a boy, George had believed he had been captured and transported by slave-traders to the end of the world, the very edge of it.

How young and foolish he had been then, before his journeys to China, and then to England and Scotland – all the countries that had helped him to grow up. But now he was grown, and he knew that at last he really *had* reached the end of the world, in this fifth part of the earth, in this wilderness called New South Wales.

He turned as someone knocked on the door. A young girl entered ... a maid by her dress. She seemed about to speak casually then stopped suddenly with her mouth open and stared at him.

'Yes?'

She looked at him with wide blue eyes. 'Are you ... George Jarvis?'

'Yes.'

'It's ... it's m'lady ... Mrs Macquarie ... she said to tell you ... her and the Governor are ready to eat luncheon.'

George nodded and smiled. 'Tell her I shall be

right down.'

As she turned to leave the maid paused and looked back at him. 'Would ... would you like me to show you the way to the dining room?'

'Yes,' George realised, 'I don't know my way around yet so that would be a help.'

The girl's cheeks blushed a bright pink, but she said not a word to him as she walked beside him down the stairs. So George asked her a question.

'What is your name?'

Her blushing deepened. 'Rachel ... I've just started as Mrs Macquarie's personal maid.'

'Just started ... so before that?'

'Well, before that, Governor Bligh, he didn't have a wife, so before that I worked for Mrs Kelly.'

'And who is she?'

'George ...' Elizabeth stood by the dining-room door looking anxious. 'George, thank goodness you have come. Lachlan has gone off somewhere with his officers leaving us to dine alone – and I need you to tell that Aboriginal boy at the window to either go away or to put some clothes on.'

George grinned and moved towards the long window, but not before he paused momentarily and looked back at the maid saying, 'Thank you.'

Rachael immediately turned and fled down the hall and out the back door over to Mrs Kelly's kitchen where she rushed up to two girls chopping vegetables at the long table and gasped out, 'I'm in love!'

'What's that?' Mrs Kelly barked, her face alert.

'What's that I heard you say, Rachel?'

'N-nothing, Mrs Kelly ... I was just saying as how I love your cooking.'

Mrs Kelly narrowed her eyes. 'And is that why you came dashing in here like a mad lunatic – to eat some of *my* cooking?'

'Yes, Mrs Kelly, I loves your cooking, so what's wrong with that?'

'Wrong? I'll tell you what's wrong with it, girl – because *you* don't work or eat in here with us no more, do you? Not now you've been promoted to be a lady's maid! Now you must take all your meals in the Governor's kitchen with his own personal cook, Mrs Ovens.'

'Oh, blimey, yeah ...' Rachel muttered, 'I forgot about that.'

Mrs Kelley put her hands on her fat hips and laughed. 'What a name, eh? A cook named Mrs Ovens? Did you ever hear the like?' She rocked with laughing delight. 'Mrs Ovens? Well, she'd better not act the snob with me, not with a name like that!'

Rachel whispered secretively to the two girls at the table and then turned and dashed out of the kitchen.

As soon as she had gone the two girls began to giggle together and Mrs Kelley abruptly stopped laughing and pounced on them, her palms flat on the table in front of them.

'Now, tell me – what did Rachel *really* say to yiz?

The girls exchanged glances then one piped up honestly. 'She said she was in love.'

'Who with?'

'We don't know. That's all she said.'

'That she was in love...' Mrs Kelly's face straightened and took on a sad expression. 'Poor cow, there's no one worth loving in this place, is there?'

Her eyes suddenly narrowed. 'Not unless he's one of them new soldiers just arrived with the Governor ... oh, my dear body and soul ...'

Mrs Kelly turned and walked heavily back to her chair. 'I'd better say a prayer for our Rachel so, because if it *is* a soldier she's got her eye on, then she'll need a prayer, and a lot more than one prayer I'm thinking.'

*

The following morning, almost every soldier, every citizen and every convict servant not assigned to a chain gang assembled on the parade ground in Sydney to hear the new Judge-Advocate, Ellis Bent, reading out the Royal Order of King George the Third who had now given to His Viceroy and Governor-General, Lachlan Macquarie, supreme control of His Majesty's dominions in New South Wales, Van Diemen's Land, New Zealand, and all adjacent Islands.'

Under the baking heat of the sun, the King's long missive seemed to go on forever ... until, at last, it ended, and the crowd's interest was renewed as the man himself moved forward to address them.

And then came the surprise and bewilderment ... his voice, everything he said to them, and the way he said it, was strange and unexpected.

To the soldiers of the New South Wales Corps who were due to be sent home, he did not express his rage or contempt for their mutiny against a former Governor, but his 'regret' at their conduct.

To the rest of the citizens, free and convict, he promised that his rule would be firm, but also fair. He asked for an end to all past dissensions and jealousies.

'Forgive, forget and look to the future,' he urged, and then quickly wiped the smiles off some of their faces by also urging them to 'show greater kindness to the native population of Aboriginals.'

Oh yes, his eyes and expression told them there was not a thing about life here in New South Wales that he had not been told about, or read about in all his papers on the colony, and again expressed his 'regret' that it should be so, but was hoping it would change.

Finally, he shocked them all again, by declaring that in his role as Governor-General – 'the honest, sober and industrious inhabitant, whether free settler or convict, will ever find in me a friend and protector.'

And on that, he left them ... wondering if he had meant even one word of it.

Chapter Nine

And as the weeks passed, he began to prove to them that he had meant it, every word he had said.

A sense of new life quickened in the colony as Lachlan Macquarie was quickly seen to be very different from his previous Governors. Gone was the gouty impatience of Gidley King, the aloof attitude of Hunter, the blasphemous rages of William Bligh. Lachlan Macquarie was down to earth, possessed a great deal of common sense and fairness, and showed clear signs of very real goodness.

He was also full of energy and zeal for practical reforms, and lost no time in getting down to work. He now viewed the colony not as a cesspit for the wicked, but as the greatest challenge of his life. Every day he was to be seen out riding with his staff, viewing his territory and noting its virtues and problems.

A fact which irritated him most of all, was that not one of the streets in Sydney town was straight. Their crookedness offended not only his eyes, but also his natural sense of order. Houses had been built in haphazard fashion, not neat, but higgledy-piggledy beside each other, some high, some low, some back, some forward ... 'What a mess!'

The biggest eyesore was St Phillip's Church, the ugliest house of worship he had ever seen, and not helped by the fact that only half of it had been constructed and the rest left unfinished.

'Check the records,' he said to Captain Antill, 'and see if there are any transported architects amongst the emancipists or convicts.'

On a ride to the outlying country districts, Lachlan's spirits brightened. Here he found well built houses, not all of just wattle and daub, but of white-washed stone; and all were surrounded by trees and neatly-kept gardens. Occasionally he found an impressive mansion that belonged to an Exclusive.

'All this land,' Lachlan said. 'Just think what could be done with all this land.'

He turned to George Jarvis who was riding beside him. 'What do you see, George? Tell me, what do you see when you look around you?'

George was looking at a roadside shack that had been nailed together haphazardly without care for detail or anything other than the provision of a shelter. A hole in the top provided a chimney and a hole in the wall served as a window. A '*no trespasing*' sign was nailed to the door.

'Well,' George replied, 'apart from a few rough houses, and a few ostentatious mansions, I see a tiny and shabby settlement surrounded by wilderness and mountains.'

'I see more,' Lachlan said. 'Oh not yet – it's too young yet, still in its infancy. But everything needed to turn this colony into a beautiful country is here, just waiting to be developed. The advantages are numerous, George. Did you notice the fine grazing lands that lie all around Sydney? And in other places the country is so thinly timbered it would take no time to clear it and erect essential buildings. A hospital would come in very handy for a start. And that eyesore of a church could be completed. And why, I wonder, is Sydney devoid of a post office? Even the smallest town in Scotland has its own post office.'

'A post office?' George smiled. 'Lachlan, this is not Tobermory or Edinburgh, this is a *convict* colony!'

'Yes, and one that still depends on its every need being shipped out from England, like a baby dependent on the milk from its mother's breasts. It's time that Sydney grew up, George, and started seeing to its own needs.'

*

Of all the inhabitants, George Jarvis was the only one who was not at all surprised when Lachlan immediately put into operation his plans to give Sydney the appearance of a regular town.

A transported architect named Francis Greenway was found, interviewed, and immediately signed up to work with the Governor and help him to bring some sort of architectural order to the crooked town of Sydney.

Patiently, George Jarvis wrote down all the orders that were then sent out to be printed and distributed for the information of all.

Any house that encroached onto the street was

to be moved back at the government's expense.

Each house was to be numbered at the cost of sixpence to the owner.

Neat fencing four feet high must front and guard all dwellings.

Footpaths for the convenience of pedestrians were to be laid on every street.

Any person found casting rubbish into the roadway would be fined.

Any pigs found wandering through the streets without a drover would be taken and slaughtered.

Any drover who brought his cattle or sheep into town then let them roam the streets while he nipped into a grog-shop would be fined. If such fine was not paid, he would be jailed.

By the time three months had passed a post-office had been established. The printing or use of promissory notes was prohibited, thereby stamping out the settlement's long habit of forgery.

Every aspect of the town was to be regulated, as was the lives of the inhabitants. Although no puritan, the new governor attempted to bring religion back to the colony. A respect for the Sabbath must be restored. Sunday was declared a day of rest. No person, either free or convict, would be allowed to perform any labour on a Sunday.

The convicts, understandably, cheered – although not quite so loudly when they learned they were to be paraded to spend one hour of that free day in church attending the morning service.

Brothels using young girls – brothels of any kind

– were no longer to be tolerated, and all proprietors of such houses would be prosecuted.

Lachlan next gave his attention to their dress. Convicts undergoing special punishment were assigned to the chain-gangs and wore regulation suits of yellow broadcloth and straw hats, but the majority, those assigned to the factories or farms, wore their own clothing. Many of the female convicts who did not possess their own clothes, and most did not, also wore government-distributed frocks of convict yellow, unless the mistress of the house they had been assigned to as servants provided them with other clothing to wear.

And since Lachlan Macquarie firmly believed that a bad appearance rarely accompanied a good life, he entreated all to pay particular attention to the neatness of their dress and personal cleanliness.

Within a week he was delighted to see a conspicuous number of female convict servants in the streets of Sydney, looking as clean and tidy as their mistresses – in some cases cleaner – with a shiny show of freshly scrubbed complexions.

*

Elizabeth and George were both beginning to worry that Lachlan was taking on too many projects and working too hard for his own good. Every hour of his day was allocated solely to the service of the colony and its people.

After two hours private work in his office after

breakfast, at ten o'clock every morning he received the reports of various civic officers, followed at eleven o'clock by military reports from his officers. Between twelve noon and two o'clock he was available to any gentlemen of the colony who wished to speak to him. Applications for Land grants would be handled on Mondays – although, as he made it clear in an announcement in the *Gazette* – he was agreeable to hear and discuss very serious or urgent matters at any time, on any day.

To Lachlan, his new position as supreme ruler of New South Wales was nothing more than a job he had been given to do to the best of his ability – a job he was eager to get on with.

And as the children of the colony seemed wholly neglected in their education, he decided that a school free to pupils would be opened immediately at Kissing Point. All parents would be expected to give it their support by the regular attendance of their children.

'And if they don't?' George asked, pen in hand, waiting.

Lachlan paused. 'I hadn't thought of that.' He shrugged impatiently. 'Oh well, if the settlers are not interested in educating their children, then their children are condemned to be fools ... I ask you, George, *what* sensible parent would not want to have their child educated?'

George sat in reflection for a moment. 'I think we must emphasise that the children's schooling will be *free.*'

'Yes – emphasise that it will *free* – what parent could refuse that? So, George ... what's next on the list?'

George glanced over at the clock. 'Bed, I hope. It's after midnight.'

'Is it?' Lachlan looked at the clock, amazed. 'Is it my imagination, or does time actually move quicker here?'

George smiled. 'I would not be surprised if it did.'

*

Before retiring to his room, George decided to take a stroll in the gardens of Government House – not that there was much of a garden – no flowers at all, just dry grass paled by the sun and the salt air from the sea, and some anaemic-looking trees with thin grey boles and skimpy foliage.

'Well, the settlement is only twenty years old,' Lachlan said the following day when George mentioned the lack of colour in the garden. 'A wilderness, George, which had to be cut back by the strength of many men before this house could even be built, let alone make a space for a garden. Still, it's a big garden in size, and the flowers can come later.'

'Come from where?'

Lachlan thought about it. 'From India, I suppose, it's much nearer than Britain ... Yes, get your pen, George, and send a letter to the British

Governor in Bengal to send as many seedlings as he can on the next ship that docks in Bengal harbour on route to this colony. Tell him to also include as many potted flowering plants as he can spare. India is saturated with flowers, like most of the East.'

As soon as George started writing, Lachlan gave him another instruction. 'Write the same letter to the British Consul in Cape Town, they have a good botanical variety there too. Then make sure it goes on the next ship that docks in Sydney heading north-west.'

George paused and looked at him, a small cryptic smile on his lips. 'And so we wonder why people assume I am your *servant*.'

'What ... oh, to blazes with what anyone thinks or says. You are part of my family, George, you know that, and *they* know that – they just don't know how or why. And how could I do all this without you? Even a lot of my officers are not as well educated as you are.'

'John Campbell is your new personal secretary, why employ him and then not use him?'

'I *do* use him, George, and he's a fine and amiable man. Tough, worldly, and he's been a great help to me so far in many ways ... but dammit, George, why should I wait an age for him to write a letter or a dispatch when you can do it for me in a few minutes? All I want is to get on with the bloody job!'

'Yes, my father.' George sighed, and continued

writing. 'But I think you should know ...' he dipped his quill in the inkpot ... 'that the editor of the *Gazette* has been complaining to me and John Campbell and everyone else that you are killing his printing machine with all your orders and instructions.'

'Oh for goodness sake,' Lachlan replied impatiently. 'Why else do we have a newspaper if not to use it to inform the inhabitants of what needs to be done? Surely it's not mere *gossip* he wants to print?'

'Yes, gossip is what he wants to print,' George said, 'because he says this colony thrives on gossip. Taking away their gossip, he says, is like taking away their food.'

Chapter Ten

In the shabby printing office of Sydney's *Gazette* newspaper, Mr George Howe, the paper's editor and printer – better known to one and all as '*Happy Howe*' – felt himself sinking with fatigue under the pile of proclamations that the new Viceroy wanted printed for the benefit of the population.

And Happy Howe was not the only one sinking under the weight: his beloved printing press was also creaking towards a collapse.

Happy finally put on his hat and set out boldly for Government House to lay his problems directly before the colony's new ruler.

It's my printing press, Your Excellency,' Happy said glumly. 'She's old and infirm, d'you see? Not up to running with the energy of a youngster anymore.'

Lachlan's immediate response was curiosity. 'May I come and take a look at it, Mr Howe? Your printing press?'

Happy Howe was utterly taken aback. No Viceroy had ever visited the office of the *Gazette* before. He paused, not sure if he liked the idea. A printer's press was like his beloved, something he cherished and something he didn't like other men touching. But how could he refuse the new governor of the settlement?

Half an hour later Lachlan was running a finger

over the old printing press and examining it carefully. 'Oh, yes, I see what you mean, Mr Howe.'

Happy nodded glumly. 'She's a good old thing. Never lets me down. But she's been here almost as long as myself, since Governor Phillip's day, and she can't cope with modern times no more. Not now Sydney needs all these new rules and proclamations.'

Lachlan considered. 'You need a new one.'

Happy sighed, blinked his eyes rapidly. 'A new one, Your Excellency? A *new* printing press?' He sighed again, stirred the papers on his desk, hummed a sob under his breath, and swallowed emotionally at the very idea.

Lachlan was highly amused by the expressions on Howe's face.

'Smile if you will, Governor Macquarie, smile if you must, but the sad fact is that the *Gazette* cannot *afford* a new printing press.'

'Then we shall just have to pay for it out of the public purse,' Lachlan decided. 'If the *Gazette* is to be the government's main line of communication to the people, then the government must financially support it.'

Happy's usual glum expression changed to one of stupefaction, his blue eyes staring with incredulity as Governor Macquarie sat down at the desk, lifted a quill, dipped it in ink and began to jot down notes for the order of a new printing press which would be immediately dispatched to England.

'One printing press ... ' Lachlan said as he wrote, and then looked up at the publisher questioningly.

'With three composing sticks,' said Happy in a shaking voice, 'two of common length, with fourteen lines Long Primer...'

Happy couldn't believe this was happening. 'Governor Macquarie ... are you sure you have not lost your wits?'

Quite sure,' Lachlan said as he wrote; then again looked at Howe questioningly.

'And 400 weight of Long Primer, with a double comp of Capitals,' added Happy. 'I've become very addicted to Capitals,' he confessed.

'Personally, I rather like italics,' Lachlan replied. 'Italics are far more impressive, do you not agree?'

'*Italics*!' Happy sang ebulliently, holding up his palms in worship. 'Oh, sir, *italics* are the very *art* of the printer! The sheer force of *drama* on the printed page! Many's the night I've actually *dreamed* in italics ... but not having any, I'm forced to come down to earth and make my point in Capitals.'

'Then we shall make even finer points with the use of italics in future,' Lachlan said, ignoring the rapturous little cries that came from the printer, '... with an equal number of italics,' Lachlan said as he wrote.

'And double primer,' Happy added, delirious. 'I don't believe any of this!'

He patted and plucked delicately at the Governor's arm to make sure he was not dreaming.

'And hackle-tooth bodkin blades with six handles.' He pointed with his finger for the Governor to write it down. 'And don't forget the quotes and exclamations!'

All written down, Lachlan sat thinking for a minute, and Happy's face returned to its normal glumness, certain that the Governor was now thinking of the cost ... having second thoughts about the cost of the wonderful new printing press with sloping *italics*.

'Why don't we have a new emblem to head the front page?' Lachlan suggested.

'A new emblem?'

'Something solid and impressive.' Lachlan narrowed his eyes thoughtfully. 'How about the Royal Arms of the United Kingdom?'

Happy almost swooned. He clutched for his handkerchief and began to mop his brow.

'Governor Macquarie ... before I came to New South Wales almost twenty years ago, I worked on *The Times* in London...' His voice began to shake with emotional little tremolos. 'And *The Times*, as you know, has the Royal Arms on *its* front page.'

'And so shall we!' Lachlan said, repeating as he wrote, 'Royal Arms of the United Kingdom, in brass, supporters couchant, about the size and form that head His Majesty's speeches to Parliament.'

Happy Howe was in a daze. Here before him, he decided, was a man who saw New South Wales as something more than just a convict colony. Here was a man with *vision!*

By the time the meeting had ended, the *Gazette* was also to have asterisks to divide its paragraphs, as well as flowers to decorate its social and gossip pages.

Turning to leave, Lachlan put his hand on the door handle, and then paused and looked over his shoulder. 'You say you worked on *The Times* in London, Mr Howe?'

'I did, Your Excellency.'

'So why did you leave such a fine newspaper to come to New South Wales to establish the *Gazette*?'

'I was transported,' Happy replied glumly.

'Ah.' Lachlan nodded his head thoughtfully – the crime had to be forgery, probably of bank notes.'

'So, newspapers are not the only things you have printed, Mr Howe?'

For a time Happy seemed unable to speak, then he looked honestly at the governor and said with a croak of nostalgia in his voice, 'In my time, Your Excellency, I have printed works of pure *art.*'

*

In the hot summer months of February and March, all the new regulations were enough to make anyone dizzy, but Happy Howe no longer complained. In his view, Lachlan Macquarie's impact on the settlement was not only fresh and healthy; it also filled everyone with a new community spirit.

'No aspect of our previously unimportant lives has failed to engage the Governor's interest,' Happy declared in the *Gazette's* gossip column, *'And never before have we had such a PATERNAL ruler.'*

Mr Hassall, a missionary, immediately wrote a letter to the editor of the *Gazette* in agreement:

> *'I'm relieved to say that the former differences between the various classes in our colony are nearly at an end and we begin to live more in peace and unity. Indeed, I don't know whether the colony could find a better man for a Governor.'*

'It's because he makes us feel as if we ain't all bad,' explained Elizabeth's maid, Rachel, as she dressed her mistress's hair for an official event that afternoon. 'Not like on the ship! On the ship the guards talked to us as if we was dogs! But Governor Macquarie, when he sees us, he don't talk to us like we was dogs, no he don't, not at all.'

Elizabeth was curious. 'How does he speak to you?'

'Well, he just says fings like "Good mornin," nice as you like, and then he walks on wivout even a spit. I always hated that on the ship – the guards spittin' at us. I always thought it was very insultin'!'

Elizabeth's eyes watched Rachel in the mirror, listening attentively as always in her efforts to absorb and understand everything about the people who surrounded her.

'It *is* insulting, Rachel. It sounds as if *they* were the ones acting like rabid dogs.'

'There now, all finished,' Rachel said, standing back to admire the work she had done on Elizabeth's hair. An' d'you know, Ma'am, I fink the sun an' sea air here in Sydney must agree wiv you. You looked as white as a ship's sail when you first come, but now yer cheeks are lookin' real peachy.'

Elizabeth moved to her feet. 'Are you joining us this afternoon?'

'What?' Rachel was completely taken aback. 'Me...? Joining you...? Oh no, Ma'am, that ain't allowed.'

'Of course it's allowed. The entire population is invited.'

'What ... all of us ... mixing together? Free 'uns and convicts alike? Even us servants?'

'Everyone.'

'But it's an official do, and Governor Macquarie and all his officers –'

'Rachel,' Elizabeth said firmly, 'it is not only Governor Macquarie's wish that everyone should attend – free *and* convict – it is also his *order*. Everyone has been given the afternoon off. Were you not informed by Mrs Ovens or Mrs Kelly?'

Rachel stared at her mistress in disbelief, and then put her hands over her mouth and started to giggle like a shocked child.

'Oh, Ma'am, that Governor Macquarie, he's a right one ain't he ... he makes up all his own rules – letting all us convicts have the afternoon off ...

the Exclusives will be so mad an' they will just *hate* him!'

'No they won't hate him,' Elizabeth said confidently, 'because Governor Macquarie consulted with them all through the *Gazette*, and so far not one has objected.'

After a moment's thought, Rachel asked quietly, 'Will ... will George Jarvis be going as well?'

'George?' Elizabeth hesitated before answering further. She was well aware now of Rachel's attraction to George, the poor girl showed it every time George walked into a room, but apart from always being his usual polite self, George seemed totally unaware of the girl and her eyes always burning on him.

'I'm sure George will be there,' Elizabeth said finally. 'Didn't I just tell you that Governor Macquarie says *everyone* must attend. Today is going to be a very special day for Sydney, so he wants us *all* to enjoy it.'

Chapter Eleven

'*Sydney is to have its first Race Meeting,*' the Gazette had cheerfully announced, "*because His Excellency the Governor has decided it will be the best method of encouraging the rearing of good horses in the colony.*'

For days the excitement leading up to the afternoon's event had kept tongues wagging and heads buzzing with excitement.

Entertainments were arranged, and for the first time in the history of the settlement, town-dweller and countryman, convict and free, all gathered for feats of fun on an open space of ground which had grandly been renamed "Hyde Park."

Convict women raced in sacks and wheelbarrows for the prize of a mound of cheese or a roll of Indian muslin.

Ladies allowed their ankles to be tied together and raced in pairs for the prize of a case of Madeira.

Then came the big event – the first official horse race in New South Wales, which Captain Ritchie won on his gelding *Chase*. His prize was fifty guineas from Governor Macquarie and a silver cup from Mrs Macquarie.

Michael Massey Robinson, a poet from Oxford who had been transported for alleged blackmail, solemnly and sonorously read a poem to the crowd, in honour of the day, dedicating it to an embarrassed Lachlan Macquarie.

'To him whose calm voice makes his people rejoice,
That this friend to Mankind is their Sovereign's
choice
And long may his mild and beneficent sway,
Enhance - whilst it sanctions the sports of today!'

Mr Hassall wrote a tactless letter to Governor King's wife who had left the colony less than three years before, telling her that she would soon learn from the public papers about how gay they had all become in New South Wales. *'It is not like the same place it was when you were amongst us.'*

But not all the inhabitants were so happy with the new Governor. Dr Reverend Arnold wrote in a complaint to England:

> *It appears to me that Governor Macquarie is of too peaceable a nature for his situation. He endeavours to conciliate all persons, and instead of showing a marked disapprobation of the emancipist–felons, he has invited some of them to dine at his table at Government House, in particular a former architect named Francis Greenway. He has also put some in responsible situations, and has made others his confidants.*

Some of the Exclusives were inclined to agree with Dr Arnold. It really was shocking – men like that architect who had once worn leg irons, not only being allowed to speak to the Governor, but also invited to dine with him! Yes, indeed, quite shocking!

But apart from these few malcontents, the rest of the population simply adored their new Governor.

PART THREE

Chapter Twelve

As First Lady of the Colony, Elizabeth took her duties very seriously. As the Governor's wife she was expected to accompany him to all official functions and social events.

For two years in a row she had hosted the customary celebrations for the King and Queen's birthdays when more than 120 guests had filled the Government House ballroom for dinner and dancing. Most of the guests considered her to be 'vivacious and charming' although some of the ladies of the devout Exclusive community considered her manner with them to be 'a little stiff'; but generally, she was liked by all.

She had also shown herself to be as energetic and full of ideas for improvement as her husband was, and had started by turning the vegetable patch in front of Government House, which had been there since Governor Phillips time, into a beautiful landscaped garden.

Elizabeth's special concern though, was the orphaned female children of the seaport's prostitutes who had been left to wander the streets in neglect and hunger.

A home was opened on the corner of George Street to protect and care for the girls so they could be housed and educated and brought up in respectability in order to prevent them from being forced into prostitution as soon as they were old enough.

She viewed many of the young convict population with compassion and genuine sympathy, seeing them as poor wretches who had not only been transported to the other side of the world for some minor crime – that was not the worst of their punishment, as she saw it – the worst was that they had been cut off from their families and all reassurances that they were still loved, that they were still human beings of value to someone.

That's when she began to understand and appreciate the value of people like Mrs Kelly and other emancipists who stayed when their time was served. And those male emancipists who were able to obtain government land grants and assigned convicts to help work their farms and holdings – these emancipists were more likely to treat their assigned convict servants with more kindness than many of the free settlers who refused to believe that any transported felon deserved to be regarded as anything more than the lowest form of human being.

It was a concern Elizabeth finally raised with Lachlan.

'This system of justice and retribution is not only badly thought out by the know-alls in Whitehall, it is very wrong,' she told him. 'When a young girl is sentenced to seven years in Botany Bay, she should be given a *return* ticket so that she can return home as soon as her sentence here is served and over. But no, all are shipped out here on a one-way ticket without any care from the government of how they will ever get back. Consequently, when their sentence is served, so many girls desperate to return home to their families have no other choice but to resort to prostitution in order to earn the money to pay for their passage back home. Is that fair, Lachlan? Is that just?'

No, it was not fair or just, yet Lachlan could not see any way to remedy the situation. Whitehall, he knew, would claim they presently had enough expense funding the war against France, so the return trip of transported thieves and villains was the least of their concerns. But he assured Elizabeth, 'I will give it some thought.'

*

A few weeks later, Elizabeth was sitting in the garden, in her favourite chair, gazing over the ocean at the far horizon above the sea, wondering when she herself would cross that horizon and see her home in Scotland again.

They had made so many plans for their Jarvisfield estate, the house, the lovely pathway up to the door, the apple and plum orchards and landscaped gardens, the improvements to so many of the tenants' houses, all now having to wait until they returned.

Before his posting to Sydney, Lachlan had been consumed with ideas for Jarvisfield, drawing up plan after plan for here and there with his architect, but now he seemed to be putting all that energy and all those ideas for improvements into the town of Sydney instead.

Still, she had no right to complain; she had willingly chosen to marry a soldier who had given good and long service to his King and country in Canada, America and India, had served as deputy adjutant general in Egypt, all resulting in him reaching the highest military and social strata in London as a staff officer to Lord Harrington and other upper-crust moguls of the British Empire in the War Office.

And they had rewarded him by sending him out to rule New South Wales – an outdoor jail filled with convicts of every age and from every part of Britain and Ireland, as well as a small community of free settlers who acted as if they owned the place.

And so much for a posting that would only last for two years, she thought. Those two years had come and gone, yet Whitehall had made no mention or move to replace Lachlan with another Governor, nor had Lachlan troubled the Colonial Office with the subject of a replacement either.

In fact, the thought of leaving New South Wales now was simply an irritating distraction to him. He had so much work still to do, so many improvements needed to make Sydney a better and more civilised place for everyone.

Elizabeth had read the dispatch he had written in reply to Lord Bathhurst who had requested a report on the state of the Colony upon his arrival in New South Wales.

> *I found the Colony barely emerging from infantile imbecility and suffering the most severe deprivations and disabilities; agriculture was languishing; commerce in its early dawn and revenue unknown. The population was threatened with starvation; the public buildings in a state of dilapidation and the few roads that were formerly built were almost impassable. People in general appeared to be depressed by poverty and neglect.*

And in the past two years Elizabeth knew her husband had succeeded in changing so much of that. He had made sure the people were supplied with enough food from the Government store, and all the architectural changes he had made had resulted in Sydney beginning to look more like a respectable town instead of a hotchpotch of a convict settlement.

Even the people seemed to have changed for the better, seemed happier, more polite and agreeable. She had overheard some of the servants saying that life in Botany might be worth living after all. And the sight of fights and the sound of curses had certainly decreased, and no one appeared to feel so depressed or bad-tempered anymore.

As Governor, Lachlan had also closed down seventy per cent of the licensed grog shops, which still left a lot open, but with fewer places for the sailors and prostitutes to hang out, the unrivalled lewdness and drunkenness of Sydney's seaport had been greatly reduced.

Elizabeth continued to gaze out over the ocean in the direction of Scotland, her face moody, her eyes hazy, due to her own private sadness. A week earlier she had suffered her third miscarriage in the two years she had been in New South Wales, and each time the loss made her think of the baby daughter she had buried in Scotland ... her sweet little Jane ...

'Missus Macquarie, milady ma'am ... begging your pardon...'

Elizabeth looked away from the blue waters of the ocean to see the Head Gardener standing with his hat in his hands and an apologetic look on his face. He was an ex-convict who had served his time but now he had been placed in charge of fifty convicts, mostly Irish, who had shown a natural aptitude for gardening and so were employed at Government House.

'May I speak to you, milady?' he asked nervously, seeing her moody expression. The free settlers of the Colony may have judged the Governor's wife as being vivacious and charming, but to the convict gardeners who worked in the grounds of Government House, her manner was always a mixture of nice but no-nonsense.

'Well?' she asked.

'Well, milady, the Governor is away at

Parramatta so I can't apply to him ...' said the gardener, glancing back at the small group of the other gardeners who were watching and egging him on.

'Apply to him for what?'

'Some time off, milady. You see, tomorrow is March the seventeenth, the feast of Saint Patrick, and some of us Irish were wondering if you would agree to give us the morning off ... so we could spend some time in holy prayer ... honouring the patron saint of our homeland.'

Elizabeth gave the gardener a small cynical smile. She doubted that time for prayer was the real reason they wanted the morning off. Most of them probably wanted to have the opportunity to spend the morning lying in bed sleeping long and late, before setting off for a tipple at one of the grog shops.

'All the other governors gave us the morning off on Saint Patrick's Day, milady,' the gardener added, and Elizabeth doubted that very much too.

'Even Governor Bligh?' she asked.

The gardener took a startled step back, knowing she had caught him out in his lie. The entire settlement knew how much Governor Bligh had hated the Irish, the Scots, the Welsh, and just about anybody else who wasn't English. And lying to the Governor's wife could get him a few whips of the lash, if not worse.

'Very well,' Elizabeth said suddenly, rising to her feet. 'The Irish convicts may have tomorrow morning off from all work, but mind – ' she warned sternly, 'every single one of you must be back at work in the rear garden of Government House by three o'clock, is that understood?'

'Oh, aye, milady, oh, yes indeed, three o'clock and not a minute after ...' The gardener couldn't believe his luck, his face rapturous with surprise and delight as he bowed his thanks to Elizabeth at least ten times before turning and rushing back to his pals to tell them the good news.

As she strolled back to the house Elizabeth watched the group of men almost dancing with delight and laughing as the gardener gave them the news – laughing like excited children at Christmas – and the sight warmed her out of her earlier melancholy.

It was time to stop moping and regain her optimism, her belief in life. She would get pregnant again and she would have her baby, one day, alive and well; but now it was time to help the Irish convicts in her service to celebrate their precious St Patrick's Day.

*

At five minutes to three o'clock the following afternoon, refreshed from sleeping late in bed and buoyed up by their tipple in the grog shop, the Irish gardeners, true to their word, returned to the rear garden of Government House and were shocked into a stunned silence of disbelief.

Rows of long tables had been laid out laden with

plates of steaming Irish stew, loaves of Irish-style soda bread, and joining at them at the tables were all the Irish maids and lads employed there.

'It's a celebration we're to have!' Mrs Kelly cried jubilantly. 'On the instructions of the mistress! Oh, didn't I tell yiz Government House would be a better place now its being run by a woman!'

The helpings of stew were huge, the warm freshly baked soda bread delicious, followed by an oatmeal pudding covered in warm sweet molasses.

'Oh, by God ...' the Head Gardener was almost in tears. 'Who would have thought ... what a lady ...'

The feast over, tankards of beer were served and all raised their drink in a toast to the Governor's wife.

'Three cheers for Mrs Macquarie! Three cheers for the Governor's lady!'

They all drank the toast, followed by expressions of disappointment. 'Bejabus,' one said, 'she's watered down the grog!'

'That's because she doesn't want yiz to get drunk,' Mrs Kelly said, knocking back the rest of her own beer. 'She don't agree with drunkenness, m'lady don't, and neither do I!'

The kitchen maids all stared at Mrs Kelly who often got drunk in the evenings, but none dared remind her of that.

More beer was brought out and Mrs Kelly continued her instructions.

'Now, we are to have one more hour or so enjoying ourselves out here, but soon as the sun drops we are all to go back inside and the gardeners to their billets. So Paddy Mahoney – how about a good old song now?'

Paddy started the singing and another convict brought out a small mouth-organ and the clapping and dancing began.

Elizabeth stood with George Jarvis by one of the open, upper rear windows of the house, both smiling as they watched the fun.

'What about the English and Scots and Welsh?' George asked. 'Are you going to let them celebrate their own saint too?'

'Yes,' Elizabeth said good-naturedly.' Let them all have their special day in honour of St Andrew, St George and St David. It's a small kindness, just one day off, and I have already informed Mrs Ovens and others of that fact.'

'Ah,' George murmured, comprehending. 'Now I understand why there have been so signs of jealousy from the others, even from the English girls serving at the tables. The Irish and their Saint Patrick have won a special day off for them all.'

Elizabeth sighed. 'They need *some* kind of reassurance, George, even if it's only the reassurance that they share the same nationality as many others who ended up here.'

'*Ello darlin!*'

Elizabeth almost jumped out of her skin as she turned round. 'Who on earth...?'

'It's Bappoo ...' George had rushed to the door. 'He must have escaped from my room.'

'Bappoo? Is he an Aboriginal? And if so what is he doing in your room?'

George returned moments later with a white parrot perched on his outstretched arm. When they reached Elizabeth the parrot looked at her curiously for a moment, and then chirped again, '*Ello darlin!*'

She put a hand to her mouth and laughed. 'George! Where did you get it?'

'It's a cockatoo. I bought him from a sailor when I was delivering letters to the captain of one of the ships. The sailor begged me to buy it because he needed money quickly.

'*Ello darlin!*'

'What are you going to do with it?' Elizabeth asked. 'We can't have it in the house, not a bird who says things like that ... the visiting ladies of Sydney would certainly not approve ... You could, of course, keep him in a cage in your room.'

'No, not in a cage,' George said firmly. 'This bird is a free settler, not a convict.'

'Then you will have to find him a place somewhere in the garden. Go down to Mr Byrne, the Head Gardener, and see if he can help you to find somewhere suitable.'

George sighed. 'If you insist.'

Minutes later Elizabeth saw George down in the garden, surrounded by the Irish servants and gardeners, all laughing as the cockatoo kept chirping from one to the other, '*ello darlin, ello darlin, ello darlin ...*

Personally, Elizabeth thought, she preferred birds that were allowed to sing their own natural songs, not birds that had been taught to talk like cockney sailors.

*

Lachlan was not a bit surprised when, a few days later, Elizabeth refused to join him on a visit to see the village that he had arranged to be built near Sydney Harbour for the Aboriginals.

'I have seen more than enough of the Aboriginals,' she said stiffly. 'The women always clothe themselves decently, so why can't the men?'

'The men will all be wearing breeches,' Lachlan assured her. 'King Bungaree gave me his word on that.'

'Nevertheless,' Elizabeth decided, 'I have enough to do today and I'm not prepared to take the risk. Perhaps, at some other time, you could arrange for me to visit ... just the women?'

'The horses are ready, sir,' John Campbell said from the doorway.

Minutes later Elizabeth watched Lachlan ride off with George Jarvis and Captain Antill each side of him, and John Campbell and the bodyguard close behind.

'Thank God for that,' she muttered to herself, turning away with relief. 'The Aboriginals are *his* pets, not mine.'

*

The Aboriginal people of Sydney lived mainly by

fishing, then selling their fish to individuals in the town. At their partly constructed new village, King Bungaree was there to meet the Governor and his staff, and watch the houses being built. He and his people had no intention of living in the new houses, preferring to sleep on the beach under the stars, but he appreciated the gesture and smiled happily when the Governor asked him, 'How do you like the houses?'

'*Murry boodgeree* (very good) Massa.'

Although the others were attempting to keep a straight face, George Jarvis's dark eyes were glistening with tears of laughter – due to King Bungaree's dress.

The Aboriginal women always wrapped themselves in cloaks of possum skins and kept their bodies covered, but the Aboriginal men walked around quite naked, without the least embarrassment, and even seemed very proud of their *natural* costume.

But Governor Macquarie had sought to remedy the matter by supplying King Bungaree and his group of males with breeches from the Government Stores. King Bungaree had been very pleased with the breeches, and now he wore them to meet his dear friend, the '*Boodgeree Massa Mawarrie!*'

Lachlan stared at the breeches dangling around King Bungaree's neck like a shawl, and attempted to ignore George Jarvis who was shaking with silent laughter.

He said sternly, 'No, King Bungaree, that is not how the breeches should be worn.'

Bungaree dandily lifted a leg of the white breeches that covered his shoulders and looked disappointed. '*Bel boodgeree* (not good) Massa?'

'Not good at all,' Lachlan said, then again insisted that he wished all Aboriginal males to wear the breeches where intended – on the lower parts of their bodies.

Two such males standing behind the king were wearing their breeches wrapped around their heads like turbans, while their bodies remained as bare as the bark on a gum tree.

King Bungaree merely shrugged up his shoulders and smilingly agreed. He was too fond of the Governor to tell him that he and his people cared as little for the breeches as they did for the houses. In the same way that he was too fond of the Governor to tell him that he was not a king – Aboriginal people had no kings or queens, only the white invaders had kings and queens – but an earlier Governor had given Bungaree the title of 'King' simply because he was an Elder and the leader of the Aboriginal people in *Koori*. The Aboriginal people cared mostly for Governor Macquarie's protection, an unusual thing, which they now flaunted in the face of any white man who dared to abuse them, retaliating with a lordly wave of the hand and shouting arrogantly, 'Go along, you damn white fellow!' Then threatening the white man with '*the jail*' and '*Massa*

Mawarrie.'

All the Aboriginals understood English very well, but only spoke it when necessary. But when they did, their English was rife with cockney slang, especially when they were driven to hard swearing, which they had learned years ago to perfection from the worst of London.

But they never swore in front of the Governor. Although their culture and language were ridiculously strange to the whites, the Aboriginals were adept at quickly summing up a person's character and anticipating his reactions in various circumstances.

King Bungaree happily invited Governor Macquarie and his massas to come to the beach and take refreshment, which in courtesy they did.

Later, when the meal was over and the evening was setting in, torch-fires were lit all around the beach and a display of entertainment was quickly ordered by King Bungeree.

Lachlan smiled his approval – he simply loved the inherent poetry in the Aboriginal ritual chants and the artistic symbolism of their dancing.

As the night wore on, the singing and chanting rose louder and louder, until it could be heard in most parts of Sydney.

This was one aspect of Macquarie that the Exclusives despised, his affectionate familiarity with the Aboriginals. His years in India had clearly debauched him. And a sad day it was for New South Wales when London sent a *Sahib* to rule them.

By now, more than two years after his arrival in the colony, there was not much Lachlan did not know about the Aboriginals and their ways.

He had learned that they possessed an amazing quickness of ear and eye, so much so that they could track a man's footsteps with perfect ease through every description of country, and although they did not appear to be even looking at the Governor, he knew they were covertly watching him and noticing his enjoyment of their performance – which led to another aspect of their nature, which was a relentless desire to show off.

War-like, they swung their waddies around their heads as they danced and sang – two of the young men becoming so competitive in their showing off they accidentally smashed their clubs together and a private fight broke out between the two.

King Bungaree, who at first fumed with anger at the two men who began to fight before their guests, quickly decided to turn failure into festivity by ordering the two men to perform their fight as an act of entertainment, for the Governor and his massas.

Lachlan immediately moved to protest, but King Bungaree patted his hand happily and urged to him enjoy it.

Astonished, the Governor and his staff sat in the warm night air and watched as the two men danced around each other with club in hand, and began to fight, bashing each other on the head until one tumbled down in an unconscious slump.

Lachlan moved to take his leave as soon as the other flourished his club in a little victory dance, before slumping down unconscious also.

'Oh, yes, *murry boodgeree*,' Lachlan agreed when King Bungaree asked his opinion of the brave fight, but George Jarvis was in quiet hysterics.

George's laughing face had attracted two Aboriginal boys aged about thirteen who ran after the delegation as they took their leave. One boy tugged on George's coat to gain his attention. `Halloo! Halloo! Top! Top! I want to peak to you!'

George stopped and turned to look at the grinning boy with long frizzy hair. 'Well?'

'I be *your* servant,' the boy grinned.

George laughed dismissively and waved the boy aside as he walked on. It was common practice in India for servants to hire other servants at a lesser wage to do the tedious work for them, but his own position was quite different. The two boys followed him, laughing excitedly.

'Halloo! Halloo! I now your servant, Massa!' the boy cried. 'I am, you know!'

'I know you are becoming a nuisance,' George said. 'Now go away.'

'I boil kettle every morning for your tea, Massa. I clean your shoes. I killit all your enemies.'

George had a feeling they would follow him all the way to Government House if he allowed them to.

I don't want or need a servant,' he said

decisively. 'Now go away – *shoo!*'

'*Shoo!*' the boys mimicked, and shrieked with laughter.

'I brush your coat every day, Massa.' The boy reached to touch the sleeve of George's blue coat. 'I catch fish for you. Halloo! Halloo, Massa!'

But George was clearly not interested. The boys looked at each other in disappointment, shrugged, and came up with another ploy.

'I *not* be your servant and go away if you pay me one shilling, Massa,' said the first boy slyly.

'I not be your servant also, Massa,' said the other boy, 'if you pay me *two* shilling.'

George smiled to himself, then swung round and grabbed the two boys and banged their heads together. 'There!' he said, rendering them dumbstruck. 'That's how we treat servants in India!'

Dazed, and each with a hand to the side of their heads, the boys looked up at George with dismay.

'Do you still want to be my servants now?' George asked.

'No, Massa.'

'No, Massa.'

George took some money from his pocket and shared it between them. 'Now go,' he said. '*Shoo!*'

'*Shoo!*' the boys mimicked, and ran back down the slope laughing.

Chapter Thirteen

With the help of Francis Greenway, the ex-convict who was proving to be something of a genius, St Phillip's Church had now been completed, and became the first consecrated building in New South Wales.

Over two-hundred-and-fifty emancipist couples living together on their government-grants of land, answered the Governor's plea and got married in the new church.

Reverend William Cowper, the junior chaplain, joyously performed the wedding ceremonies.

But Reverend Marsden, the senior chaplain, refused to participate, considering all emancipists and felons to be damned and beyond any religious redemption, as were the Aboriginals.

Instead, he applied to Governor Macquarie for the provision of enough soldiers and finances to pay for an armed expedition to New Zealand, as he cherished a fervent wish to convert the Maoris to Christianity.

Lachlan flatly refused Reverend Marsden's request, advising him to care more for his flock here in New South Wales, and to leave New Zealand's Maoris alone.

Fuming, it was a refusal that Reverend Marsden was determined to make Macquarie regret.

*

Every day Lachlan rode at least thirty to forty miles exploring his territory and making his plans, always accompanied by his military aide, Captain Anthill, and followed by his regular bodyguard of ten light horsemen under the command of Sergeant Charles Whelan.

On a cool day in September, having ridden out with Captain Antill to explore the lands around Windsor, they approached the town to see a crowd gathered at the corner of Thompson Square.

The people seemed totally engrossed in whatever was taking place.

Curious, they moved their horses forward at a walking pace until they reached the back of the crowd and a man's raucous voice reached them.

'I do hate to part with her, I do, cos she's a soft an' gentle little cow to be honest. Never makes a fuss if I have ter use the stick on her. Just takes it as her due. Now, twenty quid is what I'm asking for her. Twenty pounds. So oo's goin' to make the first bid?'

'Ten quid!' a voice shouted.

'Ten quid? Now look, this ain't a bleedin' joke! I wouldn't be sellin' me little cow at all if I weren't off to be a squatter with me few sheep. An' I *need* the money to buy a good breeding ram. One ram, five ewes, an' before yer know it, I'll have me own station an' a flock of sheep as big as John McArthur's.'

'Eleven quid!'

'Bugger off!'

'Fifteen quid!'

No one seemed to notice Governor Macquarie sitting on his horse at the back of the crowd, with Captain Antill slightly behind him.

Captain Antill's young face was stiff with disgust, but Macquarie's eyes were dark with fury.

The man was selling a woman. A pale, timid-looking young woman with a bruised face was being led around in a circle with a rope around her neck like an animal on a leash.

'Sixteen quid and a roll of cloth!' a voice offered.

'Sixteen quid an' a roll of bleedin' cloth! Gawd's breeches! Can't anyone come up with summit better'n that?'

The girl was again led round in a circle on her leash. 'Like I says, she's a soft an' gentle little cow. An' she gives good service in the straw! Let yer have it anytime yer want, especially if you keep her tame with a few whacks of the stick. Drops on her back as meek as a lamb if you use the stick.'

'Sixteen quid and a roll of good cloth, Tom Rattey. Take it or leave it. I got no more.'

'Well ... I'm being a fool to meself, I am, I am, but all right –done!'

Lachlan waited until he saw the money actually changing hands, then quickly moved forward through the startled crowd who hurtled out of the way of his horse then stood to stare at the red-coated officer.

'Blimey - it's His Ex!'

Lachlan glared at the two men. 'What in

damnation do you think you are doing?'

Neither man spoke, just gaped up at him.

'*Answer me!*' He flicked his crop across the shoulder of the astonished seller. 'Who gave you the right to think you could sell this woman in an open market like an animal!'

Tom Rattey could not grasp what all the fuss was about. He lifted a big hand and rubbed at his shoulder where the crop had stung him.

'Well, I *do* have the right to do with her what I like, Yer Excellency,' he retorted indignantly. 'She's me wife, see? Or at least she was, until I sold her to Flash here. I've done nothin' wrong, Yer Excellency. It's an unwritten law here in Botany, selling a wife. Cheaper than divorce, y'see?'

'And who instituted this unwritten law?'

Tom Rattey shrugged. 'Dunno. One bloke done it, then another bloke done the same as him. Now anyone that wants does it.'

'And do they all lead the woman around on a leash and advise their buyers to beat her with a stick?'

'Ah, no, Yer Excellency.' Tom Rattey attempted a placating laugh. 'They all know that's just part of the sales gab. Just a bit of spice to add to things, y'know.'

Lachlan looked with focused loathing into the ugly, ignorant face below him. 'So one man commits a depraved act by selling his wife like a beast, and others follow his example? Well, as it happens, I am a great believer in the use of example myself.'

By now the entire square was filled with soldiers and civilians who had rushed out to see if reports of His Excellency the Governor being in town were true.

Macquarie looked at the soldiers and beckoned them forward. 'Take that rope from the woman's neck,' he commanded.

The rope was removed.

'Now take her husband to the centre of the square, strip off his shirt, and in full view of all these people, give him ten lashes!'

A gasp went up from the crowd. Very slowly the Governor looked round the square at the people of Windsor, and when he spoke to them, a raw fury edged his words.

'A new *written* law is now going to be instituted in New South Wales. Any man who attempts to sell his wife on a leash like an animal – any man who attempts to *sell* his wife at all, will be charged under a capital offence and will suffer the severest punishment of the law!'

Other women were now comforting Tom Rattey's wife, while Rattey was tied to the flagpole in the centre of the square.

A sergeant of the 73rd stood ready, whip in hand.

Minutes later the people of Windsor saw the man who had made a public spectacle of his wife, himself being made a public spectacle of, and with every crack of the lash the women in the square cheered.

Ten lashes – it was little enough in a colony that in the past decade had seen Irish rebels and English mutineers from the Nore take more than two hundred steel-tipped lashes without uttering a sound, without letting out even a whimper, even though the skin was ripped from their blood-soaked backs – yet Tom Rattey had howled at the first strike.

'Where's yer nasty ole stick now then, Tom Rattey?' a woman shouted. 'Ow's it feel when it's you that's gettin' the beating, eh?'

Tom Rattey looked over his shoulder like an enraged bull. 'Bleedin' Governor!' he gasped through his flinching pain. 'He ain't the poor man's friend at all! He's a bleedin' brutal bastard, just like the rest of 'em!'

'Just consider yourself lucky," Macquarie said to Tom Rattey when the lashing was over, 'that the rope didn't end up around *your* neck!'

*

The news of the lashing at Windsor spread like wildfire. The lenient Lachlan Macquarie, it seemed, was not quite so lenient after all.

Many remembered the promise he had made to the people upon his arrival in the colony, that he would always endeavour *'to reward merit, to encourage virtue, and to punish vice.'*

Lachlan Macquarie's lack of leniency towards any man who had seriously broken the law and harmed others was again demonstrated when a man who had been found guilty of murder, and sentenced to death, made an appeal to the Governor for clemency.

Macquarie's refusal was brief and emphatic. 'He took life – so he shall lose it.'

The people's approval of him was now joined by an even greater respect.

Chapter Fourteen

The winter months of 1813 were dry and parched with not a drop of rain, and as a result the harvest failed. But the surplus of supplies and grain in the Government stores compensated for the shortfall.

The following year, in the early months of 1814, there was again no sign of the normal March rains. Lachlan began to watch the weather with a growing anxiety, as did the farming settlers. The colony could not cope with a failed harvest two years in succession.

'We badly need rain,' he said to Elizabeth as they prepared for a large dinner party to be held that night in Government House.

'I have a pain,' Elizabeth said quietly.

'A pain?' Lachlan turned to her. 'What sort of pain?'

'I think,' Elizabeth said, frowning as she rose to her feet, 'that you should send for Dr Wentworth and the midwife.'

He stared at her. 'Are you sure it is that kind of pain?'

'Quite sure.'

'When is the baby due?'

Not for another few weeks.'

'Not for another few weeks?' Elizabeth had suffered three miscarriages in the previous years and now the emergency of yet another miscarriage came on Lachlan so suddenly that every other thought was driven from his mind but the heartbreak and suffering awaiting Elizabeth.

In his anxiety he tried to prepare her, calm her, until in the end she lost her temper.

'Lachlan, it is *not* another miscarriage! The baby has just decided to come a few weeks early. Now, please stop behaving like Job's comforter and send for the midwife and Dr Wentworth.'

Dr Wentworth could not be found, away attending some far-flung settler. His new young assistant, Dr Redfern, came instead.

'I'll cancel tonight's dinner-party,' Lachlan said.

'No, no, it's too late for that,' Elizabeth protested. 'And it's not fair to disappoint those ladies who have spent days deciding which dress they shall wear.'

Lachlan looked unsure. 'It's only a military dinner.'

'With officers and their ladies – the worst sort to offend. No, let everything go ahead as planned and make my excuses to our guests. Although do not reveal to them the real reason,' Elizabeth added hastily. 'Just say I am indisposed due to being overtired.'

*

After the evening sun had plunged down into the sea, the invited guests flooded into Government House. Lachlan greeted them with a polite but abstracted air, the buzz of their conversation competing with the music of the small orchestra that was successfully drowning out the sounds coming from the bedroom upstairs.

Elizabeth was suffering.

At nine o'clock the party sat down for dinner. Mrs Ovens and the kitchen staff had worked wonders as always. The guests, who were totally unaware of what was happening upstairs, jollied their way through soup, roast beef and vegetables, with a third course of oysters, rounding off with pastry tartlets, pumpkin pie and fresh fruit.

No one seemed to notice that Governor Macquarie had not eaten a bite. All were unaware of the terrified suspense being endured by their host. He had completely forgotten the reason for this 'official' dinner, which was beginning to seem interminable.

A number of times George Jarvis slipped into the room to whisper the latest news into his ear. And George whispered the truth, as Lachlan trusted him to do. Elizabeth was suffering badly, but Dr Redfern seemed to think it was all quite normal and there was no cause for worry.

The clock in the hall loudly chimed out the hour of midnight, and for some strange reason the entire room seemed to go quiet.

A few seconds later all heads turned curiously at the sound of frantic feet clattering and skidding down the stairs into the hallway.

George Jarvis slid to a stop at the open door of the dining room, his eyes staring at Lachlan, his breath caught in his throat.

'A son!' he eventually gasped. 'A strong and healthy son!'

Everyone stared at George, then at the startled Governor, then at each other.

Goodness! So that was why His Excellency was so irritable tonight! All this time while they had been dining, his wife had been going through the labour of childbirth upstairs.

Again all eyes turned to the Governor, who seemed to be finding the news that he had a son too incredible to believe.

All ears listened ... then it came - the sound of a baby crying ... a sound that grew stronger and stronger until Lachlan suddenly sprang out his chair and raced up the main staircase with George Jarvis following.

The guests excitedly surged after them, the ladies squealing with delight. Now the party would go on all night. 'Wine! Wine!' somebody shouted. 'More wine all round to toast the baby's health!'

Servants appeared from every door and archway, all surging towards the main staircase.

As Lachlan and George reached the landing, Mrs Reynolds, the midwife, another ex-convict, came out of the bedroom with beads of perspiration still glistening on her flushed face.

'Tes a boy we got for thee, sur! 'Andsomest little boy as I ever did see! And thur an't nuthin' wrong with 'is lungs! Hark at 'im now, screeching like a tyrant!'

When Lachlan entered the bedroom, young Dr

Redfern was pouring hot water into a basin and washing his hands. His coat was gone and so was his neckcloth. The sleeves of his shirt were rolled up to the elbows. He looked tired but triumphant as he turned and smiled with satisfaction.

'I told you there was no cause for worry. I knew we would win through in the end.'

Lachlan smiled in gratitude at the young doctor who had once worn leg-irons.

Elizabeth was sitting up in bed, purring over the child in her arms like a cat with her kitten, clucking away as if her ordeal had never been.

Jubilant, she looked up at her husband and smiled.

Lachlan looked at the newly washed naked infant. There was a knot of golden hair on his head. ... Oh yes, he was a Macquarie.

Elizabeth took the shawl that Mrs Reynolds handed to her and wrapped it around the baby. 'Thank God there are no freezing Perth winters here to take a child,' she said quietly ... and then she looked up and smiled at the amazed expression on her husband's face as she handed him the boy.

'Lachlan Campbell Macquarie,' she said, before he even asked.

*

The most surprising and moving event that followed the *Gazette*'s announcement of the birth was the stream of emancipists that came bearing gifts for Governor and Mrs Macquarie's baby son.

One old swag brought his pet parrot that he had trained to talk. 'No curse words, mind,' he told the Governor, 'nothing like that. No, that's why I thought the little lad might enjoy chatting to him, when he gets a bit older, like.'

Another came with a baby kangaroo. Another arrived with a stuffed Emu. Even the convict girls came with little items of clothing and woolly toys, which they had sat up through the nights making with wool they had filched from the wool factory where they worked.

'Oh, that is kind,' Lachlan said with suppressed emotion as George Jarvis brought more knitted gifts from the girls to him.

When Elizabeth saw the little bonnets and booties and beautifully knitted woollen jackets, tears began to slip down her face.

'And look at this!' She held up an extremely stylish little sailing boat that a group of Irish convicts had carved and painted.

'They wouldn't do it if they didn't like him,' Mrs Kelly told Elizabeth. 'The convicts wouldn't give a tinker's curse about the Governor having a new child if they didn't like the Governor himself. But they do, we *all* do – except for the Exclusives, of course. They hate him something fierce!'

Perplexed, Elizabeth frowned. 'But *why* do they hate him, Mrs Kelly, do you know?'

'Aye, I do, m'lady. That small group of rotters hate him because of the way he treats the convicts and emancipists. He doesn't treat them like scum, does he? No, he treats the cons fairly and then when they've served their time he gives the emancipists a chance to better themselves. Sure wasn't your own little lad delivered by young Dr Redfern.'

'Yes.' Elizabeth sat thoughtful. 'Why was Dr Redfern sent out here, do you know? What crime did he commit?'

Mrs Kelly huffed and puffed before finally exclaiming, 'Ah, sure, it was nothing more than a bit of foolishness, m'lady. He had just finished his studies at the school of medicine in London and he and his student friends were celebrating and they all got a bit tipsy, and when the others dared young Dr Redfern to dress himself up as a highwayman in a mask and ride out and pretend to be a robber – he did so, just for the fun of it – and got caught.'

Mrs Kelly nodded her head at the sadness of it. 'Daft it was – a daft dare and a stupid joke – but none of his friends were laughing when he was sentenced to be transported for seven years hard labour in Botany Bay.'

'A highwayman? No, it was Dr Wentworth who wore a mask and rode out as a highwayman,' Elizabeth said. 'I remember him telling me quite truthfully about the event that brought him here.'

'Well, I'm almost certain that young Dr Redfern was a highwayman too,' said Mrs Kelly. 'And if you're asking *me* what he did to get sent out here, then you don't know, so he *could* have been a highwayman, couldn't he?'

Elizabeth flicked Mrs Kelly a cynical glance. 'What, *two* highwaymen, and both just happen to be doctors?'

'Well ...' Mrs Kelly was getting flustered, 'maybe it's just something that doctors like to do, m'lady, dress all in black and pretend to be highwaymen, and then maybe they didn't do anything wrong at all and were falsely charged, like so many of my kitchen girls were. But Dr Wentworth and young Dr Redfern are the only two doctors we have in the entire colony, and so whatever the reason, its very lucky for us that the two of them *did* get sent out here to Botany Bay and not to anywhere else, isn't it?'

Elizabeth looked down at her newborn son, delivered so perfectly by young Dr Redfern. 'Yes, very lucky for us,' she agreed.

*

For days, Lachlan's mind had been preoccupied with wondering what nationality his son would be? A New Hollander? A New South Welsh? A Botany Bayist? Even worse – that he should be known as a *currency* child!

The name of being a *currency* child was given to all those children born here in the colony, due to the fact that the colony's currency was inferior to the British pound sterling. Consequently anyone born here was known to be *currency*, as opposed to those born in the Mother country who were regarded as pure *sterling*.

Even while visiting the new school, he had heard this weapon of snobbery being used amongst the children in the playground. 'You cheeky brat! How dare you turn up your *currency* nose at me! I am pure *sterling*, and that I'll have you know!'

What this country needed, Lachlan decided, was a new name. A name that would bring the people together under their own national identity. A name encompassing everyone; those born of the British regimental class, free immigrants and emancipists alike. A name they could all be proud of.

A name that he found when the Colonial Secretary, in London, Lord Bathurst, sent him copies of the charts of the continent of *New Holland* made by the explorer Captain Matthew Flinders.

Like many explorers Flinders had noted the stars of the southern constellations, using the arms of the Southern Cross as pointers to the stars of the *aurora astralis* in the skies around the South Pole.

'Aurora astralis ...' the words fascinated Lachlan and floated across his mind and across his notepaper with his pen until he finally decided on the word he liked best.

Excitedly, Lachlan immediately wrote a reply to Lord Bathurst acknowledging receipt of Flinders' charts of Australia.

'I have chosen this name of Australia,' he wrote, 'which will I hope be the new name given to this country in future, instead of the

*name hitherto given it of "New Holland,"
which, properly speaking, applies only to a
very small part of this immense continent.'*

A new *General Order* was written to be read out to
all soldiers writing home in the future, as well as a
proclamation from the Governor printed in the
Gazette informing all citizens of *'The new name of
this new country...'*

'Australia,' read Mrs Ovens. She looked up from
her newspaper. 'It has a nice ring to it, don't you
think so, Joseph?'

Joseph Bigg shrugged his shoulders. 'It'll never
be used,' he replied dismissively. 'No one will put it
on their letters for their new address. Specially the
soldiers won't.'

'Why not?'

'It's too hard to remember, it's too bleeding long,
and it's too bloody hard to spell.'

'Oh, I see ...' Mrs Ovens bowed her head and
smiled shrewdly. She was certain now that Joseph
Bigg could not read nor write, let alone spell a
word as long as Australia.

Chapter Fifteen

Although ruled by a soldier, Sydney was becoming more and more like a well-regulated civilian town. But in order for it to function efficiently, there were a number of civic posts that still needed to be filled.

Yet Lachlan found, to his dismay, that the only freely come persons to the colony that had any administrative or executive ability were his own officers. So, without qualm, he continued to seek men of capacity and merit within the emancipist community to fill these positions.

In quick succession a number of emancipists were appointed to civic and government posts, including the appointment of Simeon Lord and Andrew Thompson as magistrates.

Reverend Samuel Marsden was apoplectic when he found he was expected to sit on a committee with two emancipists. He faced the Governor armed with the wrath of God.

'You expect *me* to join my priestly name with these two men whose characters are notorious for improprieties!'

'Yes, I do,' Lachlan replied calmly. 'And they are *not* notorious characters, as you well know. Simeon Lord was sent out here at the age of nineteen for a crime so insignificant it is not even in the records. Since then his behaviour has been exemplary.'

'Say what you will of Simeon Lord, he is still a former convict. And as for the other one, Andrew Thompson, he is even worse! His crime was *political!*'

'Of political origin, yes. He burned a landlord's haystack at the age of sixteen and served seven years in Botany Bay in retribution. Those seven years are gone, Reverend Marsden. The debt has been paid.'

Reverend Marsden shook his head stubbornly. 'I would find it totally incompatible with my sacred functions to sit on any committee with two men who have worn leg-irons. It would be a degradation of my office as senior chaplain of the colony!'

Lachlan regarded him coldly. 'I am well aware, Reverend Marsden, that you have been sent out here in a *religious* capacity. But if you continue to regard emancipists with condescension and contempt, then I see you serving little purpose to the majority of the population. If we cannot expect humanity and some small degree of *charity* from a Christian priest, then who – in God's holy name – can we expect it from?'

Reverend Marsden swept imperiously out of Government House, muttering his fury. If Macquarie thought he could order the saints to mix with the sinners then he would find himself facing a holy war in New South Wales.

*

Reverend Marsden's holy campaign started the following day. He visited all his Exclusive parishioners, confiding to them in tones of pious despair the fears he was beginning to harbour about Governor Macquarie's 'peculiar system.'

'He is trying to unite the free and convict population,' Marsden said. 'Like goats and sheep.'

Weeks later he was still murmuring his fears, although when speaking to those Exclusives he knew to be somewhat less than devout, he edged his words on a different vein, that would cut just as deep.

'He is trying to raise one class and lower the other. He is trying to bring the bonded and the free to a common level.'

Now he had stirred it, the reaction was just as Reverend Marsden hoped it would be. Even those who had happily mixed with all classes in the open air on Sydney's first Race Day, were now beginning to see underlying currents of evil and destruction in Macquarie's system. All agreed that some of his policies were totally unacceptable and had to be stopped.

They formed a delegation and made their way to Government House, voicing their displeasure to Governor Macquarie, very candidly.

Lachlan, however, had never been impressed with this small pompous group of mock gentry, believing that any true *gentleman* doing well in England would not need to leave it to do better elsewhere – especially in a convict colony on the other side of the world.

He forbore patiently with all the complaints of the Exclusives, but as conciliatory as he was reputed to be, they soon discovered he was not to be bullied.

They hastened to agree with him that those convicts who had served their sentence should, indeed, have a place in the future of the colony, but not, definitely *not* on the same footing as themselves – a class of superior society who had *never* committed any crime.

The emancipist's role, as they saw it, should be a penitent one of labouring and serving the gentry, whatever their former occupation might have been.

Governor Macquarie begged to differ. 'It is my intention,' he said firmly, 'to make this colony an effective member of the British Empire to which it owes its existence. And to that end I intend to call forth *all* the energies of the colony, for the benefit of *all* its inhabitants.'

When they sought to argue further, sought to remind him sternly that he was a soldier of the *Crown* and not – surely not – an advocate of the democratic principles of the *French* revolution, he smiled at them coolly, but his eyes held the light of battle. Lachlan Macquarie's weakness for standing by the underdog, which had first started in the West Indies, and then grew in India, was now flowering into a full-blown obsession in New South Wales.

'In this Colony,' he said, 'there are seven

thousand inhabitants, out of which only *one hundred and sixty* are settlers who have not been former convicts. You are only a mere handful of the population – yet you *demand* not only the cream, but all of the milk as well!'

He shook his head positively. 'No, sirs, you shall *not* have it all! Not while I head the government here. The emancipist who has served his time *must* be given a chance to benefit from his own good conduct and return to his former place in society. The convict, too, must *also* see a chance to benefit from his own good conduct – otherwise why should he ever abandon bad conduct – if it's going to profit him *nothing?*'

They were stunned by his anger.

He made it clear that he would not be dictated to by the whims and greed of any free settler who wished to grow rich on the toil of convict and emancipist labour.

'And neither,' he added vehemently, 'will I allow a convict sentenced to seven years, upon completion of such sentence, to find himself penalised for *life!*'

As the delegation of angry Exclusives left Government House, George Jarvis stood by the window and watched them go, regarding them with his usual unruffled interest.

Why, he wondered, was it only small-minded men who sought self-gratification from power over others? Why the petty need to destroy and lay waste the hopes and dreams of other men while in their own pursuit of grandeur?

And these men – these so-called Exclusives – with their need to sit in high places and domineer others, men who ruled over houses filled with free convict servants who did all the work and called them 'master', who would these Exclusives be back in Britain – *without* their free servants – *without* their free land granted to them by the government?

Most had arrived in the colony with very little money, and even less intelligence – not all, but many whom he had met. Yet once here, in possession of all their free government gifts, they demanded even more special privileges and authority, demanded to be regarded reverently at all times as one who is above the common herd of less fortunate men.

George turned from the window and looked at Lachlan. '*Nabobs*,' he said with a half smile.

Lachlan nodded, placing papers in the drawer of his desk. 'Nabobs of the worst kind, George. What they have gained for themselves, they don't want others to gain also.'

Lachlan was still fuming at the group whom he considered as no more than the trumped-up bogus aristocracy of New South Wales. They came here, desperate to gain the land and lifestyle that would have been beyond their reach and status in England, and now they had achieved that lifestyle and grand houses built by convicts, their desperation to prevent any attempts by the emancipists to achieve the same advancement and privileges displayed nothing more than the pathetic snobbery of *upstarts.*

He himself had mixed and moved amongst some of the leading and wealthiest households in England's aristocracy where good breeding and true gentility could be seen as fact; but even the most haughty of those would have been shocked and disgusted by this ruthless clawing by the Exclusives to get their hands on everything that could be got, while refusing anyone else to reach the same pinnacle of privileges as themselves.

Even back in Britain, the unfairness of the aristocratic system was softening and slowly changing, but here in New South Wales it was hardening to a level that was laughable, although it wasn't funny. These were the new pioneers of the new Australia, this greedy and self-interested bunch of malcontents.

'Why do they call themselves Exclusives?' George asked.

'Because although they will happily participate in *trading* with emancipists in business they would rather die than allow them any rights on a social level.'

'They are fools,' George decided.

'Of course they are, George. When an army advances, *all* the soldiers march forward, not just the top-ranking officers and generals – and the same goes for a country and its people.'

*

While the Exclusives gathered to gossip and seethe, Lachlan ignored them and got on with his work.

For some time he had been giving thought to Elizabeth's concern that many young convict girls, on completion of their sentence, were forced to turn to prostitution as the only means of earning their fare back home; and now he had come up with a solution – not a perfect solution – but the only one he could think of.

He took Francis Greenway, his architect, out to the site he had chosen away from the busy city in the more airy and open land at Parramatta, and discussed with him the specifications for his new project.

'What we need, Francis, is a very large house to be built right here – a house as large as a hospital would be – with enough ground at the back and sides of the house to make a few suitable gardens.'

'For what purpose?'

'For the purpose of giving the girls a safe home to live in after they have completed their sentences.'

Francis Greenway said hesitatingly, 'But what good is that, if all the girls want to do is get back home?'

'Yes, I've thought of that,' Lachlan replied, walking away and measuring the distance with each pace he made.

'And here,' he said, stopping and turning, 'just a short walk away from the house – we will build a new wool factory for the girls to work in. Many of them work in the old wool factory anyway, but that is part of their punishment.'

Greenway was still puzzled. 'So what difference will working in this new factory be? It's a way of getting back home the girls want.'

'Exactly,' Lachlan nodded. 'And when they become emancipated and receive their freedom, the girls can live safely in the house *there,* and work safely in the factory *here,* producing wool for the government to sell abroad – and getting *paid* for their work – enabling them to earn enough money to pay for their passage home, without having to resort to prostitution at the docks.'

'Well I never ...' Francis Greenway thought it was a wonderful idea.

'Do you think you could get the plans drawn and all the work done in three months?' Lachlan asked. 'The need is becoming very urgent.'

'Three months?' Greenway grinned. 'I'll give it a fair go, but I'll need more than one gang of convicts assigned to do the building work.'

And as England was continuing to send ship after ship filled with convicts out to the colony, and as it was Lachlan's duty to find them employment, he told Greenway, 'You can have as many gangs as you need. but you *must* make sure that all overseers remember the new rule – no unnecessary use of whips by the overseers, and no floggings are to be carried out unless the crime warrants it and is therefore ordered by a magistrate.'

As they walked back to their horses Francis Greenway felt bound to say, 'The Exclusives are furious about it, you know, Governor Macquarie? This new rule of yours that forbids flogging without the order of a magistrate. They cannot see how a master can maintain order in his own home, nor obedience from his convict servants – if he's not allowed to use the whip.'

Lachlan paused to think about that, and then shrugged. 'If a man needs to use a whip to keep order in his own home, then he's not much of a man or a master.'

And knowing Governor Macquarie as well as he knew him now, Francis Greenway knew that was the end of the subject.

Chapter Sixteen

The house for emancipated females and the new wool factory was completed. The first proper road from Sydney to Parramatta had been built.

The entire area of Parramatta was reshaped and reformed, new streets and avenues were mapped out and given names. Every district, the Governor insisted, must have a main thoroughfare and a grass common.

Meanwhile, other convicts were occupied with completion of the road from Sydney to Windsor; and the Sydney to Liverpool turnpike road was in full progress. In the town of Sydney itself, the foundations for a new hospital were being laid.

In the harbour, a convict ship had arrived pouring five hundred more convicts into the settlement, while others who had completed their sentence were freed.

None of the new emancipists had the money to pay their passage home – transportation to the antipodes was always supplied with nothing more than a one-way ticket, no matter how short or long the sentence. So they applied to the Governor for a licence to set up in business as tradesmen, blacksmiths, carpenters, bakers and butchers, in accordance with their former occupations, while the rest applied to the Governor for a land grant in order to become farmers.

No licence or land was ever granted by Lachlan

Macquarie without a lecture – informing the applicant that he expected good industry and good conduct – otherwise he would take the licence or the land back.

And with each land grant he released, Lachlan saw the land being cleared and the colony extending in size. The emancipists settlers were industriously making this land their own, and it filled his heart with satisfaction just to watch them.

In his private life, too, Lachlan was finding happiness in New South Wales. Elizabeth had proved to be his greatest source of strength, his loyal confidante, his most ardent supporter.

In the drawing room at Government House he found Elizabeth sitting in the evening sunlight by one of the long windows, absorbed in a book. He had been away for two days examining the area around George's River. As always her face brightened into a smile when she looked round and saw him.

'Elizabeth,' he said good-humouredly, then a figure in the garden caught his eye and his expression lost all jest. He moved to the window and gazed out.

'Oh, George ...' he said quietly. 'I sometimes think he feels as out of place here as he did in England and Scotland.'

Elizabeth leaned forward and saw George Jarvis sitting alone on a bench in the garden.

'I would not have said he feels out of place,' she said honestly. 'He seems quite content in his day-to-day life. He is always busy and goes almost everywhere with you.'

'Yes, but that is his work. What of his private life?'

'I believe he could have his pick of the maids.'

Elizabeth had learned this from Mrs Ovens, who had confided that a number of the maids found George very attractive and one had even written a love-letter to him.

'And George?' Elizabeth had asked. 'How does he respond to the maids?'

'Oh such airs! Such graces!' Mrs Ovens had rolled her eyes and laughed. 'He's always nice and polite to me, of course, and, well, I like the young man myself, but if you ask me he's too good-looking by far. And although it's not my place to say it, George Jarvis is far too aloof for his own good!'

The maids – you mean the convict girls?' Lachlan asked with a frown. 'No, don't answer that, I don't want to know anything more.'

Lachlan returned his gaze to the garden and George Jarvis who, in turn, was gazing at the world as he always did, with unruffled interest.

Over the years George had changed from the boy he had been in India into a reserved young man. It was as if his education in Britain had changed his entire perspective on life and opened him up to a world of serious thought.

But his innate sense of humour remained.

Even now, dressed in his tailored suits with only

a trace of white silk at the neck and cuffs, and always looking neat and perfect, he would still pass visitors in the wide hall of Government House and respond to their questioning look with a quiet smile as he joined his hands in an exaggerated salaam, as if to say, Yes, I am a brown-skinned Arab, from India, and allowed to stroll through Government House as if I lived here! *Curious*, isn't it?

Ever polite, he was never humble.

George Jarvis now seemed to view the world and its pretensions with a look of silent amusement, and apparently felt no attachment to anyone, except Lachlan. But even with Lachlan, he could be reserved and remote.

Lachlan sighed. 'In his young days, in India, George was always so full of laughter, so full of mischief and fun. The tricks he would pull on Bappoo and drive the poor man mad ... yet Bappoo adored him, wept his eyes out when George left with me for England ... maybe that was my mistake, taking George from the East to the West.'

'And now he is in neither the East or the West but in the South,' Elizabeth said. 'His loyalty to you has brought him a long way.'

'To a convict colony ...' Lachlan sighed again, the old worry back in his heart. 'It would distress me if I thought George was unhappy, but at times it's hard to know what he is even thinking, let alone feeling. I wonder what does he think? About his life? His future? At times, he is like a sadhu.'

'What is that?'

'A holy man, in India, who spends long hours in silent reflection.'

Oh, yes, I agree with you there.' Elizabeth murmured, having decided long ago that George Jarvis, for all his agreeable good nature, was as deep as a well.

Chapter Seventeen

For the third year running there had been no winter rain.

July and August came in with occasional dews, but no rain. The harvest looked destined to fail again.

Through the *Gazette*, Lachlan issued numerous General Orders instructing the people to conserve all their grain. Heads of household were advised to ration their families to only so much bread per week as could be made from a gallon of wheat and a gallon of corn. This way the small farming settlers could survive if the harvest failed totally.

The bushels of wheat in the Government stores, which he had been delighted to reduce from ten shilling a bushel to eight, now rose to nine shillings.

By Christmas, all the rivers were drying up. The grass was parched and the hungry cattle were unable to pasture. By the end of December 1814 large numbers of sheep and cattle had perished. The colony was facing the worst famine it had ever known. And all looked to Governor Macquarie to save them from starvation.

There was not enough time to seek help from the Mother Country: a consignment of grain and food supplies would take too long to reach them. So once more Lachlan looked towards India.

He wrote to the Governor of Bengal requesting

that two hundred and fifty tons of wheat be shipped to New South Wales with the greatest speed.

Through the *Gazette* he pleaded with the large landowners and settlers who had their own hidden hoards of grain to bring them to the King's Stores for sale to the Government.

His plea fell on deaf ears.

The supplies in the King's Stores were getting lower and lower. The price of wheat rose to fifteen shillings a bushel.

Governor Macquarie's pleas to those hoarding hidden supplies of grains turned into threats.

He warned that unless they offered their supplies to the Government, he would resort in future to buying all grain needed for the King's stores from India at half the price, and when the drought was over they would find no market in New South Wales for their expensive local grain.

He issued a proclamation that was not only published in the *Gazette*, but also ordered to be read out in all squares and districts, no matter how far from the metropolis.

Settlers – especially those who are in opulent circumstances, principally owing to the assistance they have received from the bounty of the Government in originally granting them lands, stock, provisions and convicts to help them cultivate their grounds, ought to have been the first to

*come forward at such a time to supply
Government with such grain as they could
conveniently spare, and at a reasonable and
moderate price.*

All to no avail. The Exclusives were waiting until
the price rose even higher.

*

A ship was spotted turning round the South Head
of the harbour. It was the grain from Bengal!
Eagerly everyone ran down to the harbour to cheer
it in. Amongst them was the Governor who stood
waiting with a smile of relief.

But the ship's cargo was not the tons of Indian
grain. It was another shipment from England of
five hundred more convicts, all in dire need of
being fed.

And with the convicts came another batch of
adventuring 'emigrant' settlers – come to take
advantage of the land grants and free labour that
New South Wales offered to those who wanted to
make a quick fortune to take back to Britain. Very
few of them had any worthwhile skills to offer the
colony, all depending on the convicts to do the
work for them.

Lachlan fumed.

'These people are useless to the colony,' he wrote
home to the Colonial Office, 'completely *useless*!'

Chapter Eighteen

'*These people are human beings too,*' the girl cried indignantly, '*and probably a lot more honest than you are!*'

The girl's voice made John Campbell turn away from the captain and look at the row of female convicts lined up on the ship's deck. All were unwashed and unkempt ... but there was something about the girl's voice, and the way she held her head high ... and that splendid hair .... unkempt of course, hanging down around her shoulders, but still managing to shine golden here and there under the sun's rays.

'Quiet, you whore,' a sailor snapped.

'Don't you *dare* call me a whore!' the girl retorted, tears now glistening in her eyes. 'Oh, the humiliation of this!' she cried, 'Being made to stand for inspection like cattle at a fair!'

'Keep that girl quiet!' the captain called irritably, then turned his attention back to John Campbell who had come on board to find some male convict servants to work in the stables at Government House.

'We have some strong young men in this batch,' and some with the appearance of good breeding too,' said the captain, leading the way to where the male convicts had been grouped. 'Good breeding turned bad I daresay.'

But John Campbell was not following the

captain, he was still standing looking towards the girl with the golden hair. Tears were running down her face now and he could see she was very young, no more than seventeen.

It was unusual to see a female convict so emotionally affected by her circumstances ... after the long voyage most were so beaten and weak in mind and body that the only reaction they could manage on finally reaching land was either tired indifference, or an expression of brazen sullenness.

But this girl looked humiliated ... utterly humiliated by being made to stand in a line-up.

Boats had been rowing out to the ship as soon as it had anchored, many carrying Exclusives looking for new servants, and once on board they could take their pick.

A middle-aged woman in a black dress and bonnet stepped aboard, looking to all the world like a widow in her weeds or some prim rector's wife, but John Campbell recognised her for who she was – Mrs Hester, the proprietress of a brothel in Sydney who had been warned many times but still came aboard every ship that docked, looking to procure young girls as 'servants' – but not today, John Campbell was determined the evil witch would procure no young girls today.

Unsurprisingly, she had headed straight for the girl with the golden hair and had already asked her a question when John Campbell strode over to them.

'I'm eighteen,' the girl was replying.

'And not for your establishment, Mrs Hester,' said John Campbell sharply, cutting in. 'Now how many times have you been warned – *no bloody soliciting of young girls sent into Governor Macquarie's care!*'

'I was merely looking for a new housemaid,' Mrs Hester declared indignantly, ' and she *is* over sixteen, Mr Campbell, she has just told me so.'

'And now *I'm* telling you to bugger off back to your stinking brothel! And the next time I catch you on one of these ships I'll report you to Governor Macquarie and next time he *will* have you prosecuted – unless of course it's the ship that'll be taking you home to the back alleys in Billingsgate.'

Mrs Hester fired a dark look of venomous hatred at John Campbell, before turning away towards the roped chair that would lower her back into her boat.

'*You and Governor Macquarie can go and sod yourselves!*' she shouted viciously, seconds before the chair was lowered.

The girl was looking utterly bewildered when John Campbell turned back to her. 'Surely she was not ...'

'Never mind her. Now, your voice, miss ... you sound as if you have had some education,' Campbell said. 'Mrs Macquarie would appreciate that, and a new maid is needed at Government House.'

'You mean ...' the girl's blue eyes opened wide in

disbelief, 'I would be a maid to the *Governor's* wife?'

'Well no, you would have to do your apprenticeship with Mrs Kelly or Mrs Ovens first ... until we find out what type of girl you are. Now then, stay here and don't move, I need to find some suitable stable boys before we go ashore.'

Later that day, John Campbell gave the girl's papers to Elizabeth. 'I think she could make a decent housemaid,' he said.

'And what makes you think so?' Elizabeth queried, although she knew John Campbell was always very shrewd in his selection of any convicts who worked in the Governor's household.

Campbell hesitated. He had personally selected the girl because her voice and golden hair had attracted him, in a fatherly way, and because she appeared the type who might prefer to drown herself overboard than be seduced into prostitution by a guard or a seaman on the voyage out from England – as well as appearing suitably intelligent enough to serve as a maid in Mrs Macquarie's personal employment.

'She has some dignity in her manner,' he replied, 'and she seems bright enough.'

Elizabeth was frowning as she read the girl's papers. 'And where is she now?'

'Getting bathed, m'lady. You know Mrs Kelly won't allow any convict from a ship into her kitchen until they have had a bath first.'

Elizabeth nodded. 'Well, as soon as she is clean,

tell Mrs Kelly to send the girl up to me.'

And that was how the beautiful young English girl, Mary Neely, walked into Government House and the life of George Jarvis.

Chapter Nineteen

'I strangled her – my mistress,' Mary said to her awe-struck audience in the kitchen. 'I put my hands around her throat and squeezed the life out of her. She's dead now, ten feet under, and it surely is the kindest place for her to be. She had a friend, another nasty piece like herself, with red hair and sly eyes whom she called "Louise", and I would have liked to strangle her too, but I never got the chance. Still, my day with her friend Louise may yet come! When I go back!'

Mrs Kelly was looking mighty uneasy. 'Look here, Mary Neely, I don't know if I like having a murderess in my kitchen!'

'Well you *hate* thieves!' Mary challenged. 'So pray tell us, Mrs Kelly dear, what crime of a convict *is* acceptable in your kitchen?'

The maids were all staring at Mary with a look akin to reverence. In the space of three weeks she had won the affection of Mrs Macquarie and had got herself elevated to service in the mistress's private apartments, and now she was daring to challenge Mrs Kelly in her own kitchen!

'*Innocence!*' Mrs Kelly declared. 'That's what I like in my kitchen. *Innocence!* Or politics. There's nothing wrong with politics. But all these other girls here in my kitchen are innocent. That they are! All innocent as babes.'

Mary laughed, musically. 'All convicts in New

South Wales are innocent, according to you! Well here is one that is most definitely *not* innocent. I am guilty of murder. As true as my hand I am!' She held up a slim white hand that did not look capable of strangling anyone.

'I was never one for violence myself,' said Mrs Kelly. 'Not even in the heat of passion is it right...' She pushed uncomfortably at her cap as she remembered the betrayal of her lover.

'A person,' said Mrs Kelly, 'a *good* person, may find themselves in a temper and lashing out with a plank in the heat of rage, and there may be some evil souls who would call that *attempted* murder. But there is something about the deliberate taking of life that is evil through and through!'

'She did me a terrible wrong,' Mary insisted hotly, 'and I vowed that vengeance would be *mine!*' Her blue eyes moved over the awe-struck girls. 'Even now, every night, I take out the Black Queen from my pack of cards and work dark magic – like the Aboriginals' voodoo – on my former mistress.'

'Who says the Aboriginals do voodoo? Not here in Botany they don't!' exclaimed Mrs Kelly. 'And what use is your Black Queen and all that magic business – if the poor woman is dead!'

Mary lifted her chin and looked at the cook as if she was a simpleton. 'The witch may be dead – but I am *not* finished with her yet!'

And with that she flounced out of the kitchen with all the haughtiness of a queen, for now being employed *upstairs*, she ate her meals in the

171

kitchen of Mrs Ovens.

When the meal was served on the table, Mrs Ovens sat herself down to enjoy the nonsense of Miss Mary Neely. Never had the kitchen been so alive or such fun since Mary had entered it. The girl was beautiful, fascinating, adorable, although you could not believe one word she said.

'I'm not lying,' Mary was saying to the other servants as she broke a piece of bread in her hands, 'I lay in my bed night after night thinking of them, my black-haired witch of a mistress and her red-haired friend with the sly eyes. She hated me because I wouldn't kow-tow to her overblown opinion of herself. Oh yes, a right pair of witches they were...'

'Two nasty bints, if you ask me,' said a maid.

Mary nodded. 'The two of them – they weren't worth *that!*' She snapped her fingers with a display of condescension.

Mrs Ovens shook her head over her stew in secret mirth. The girl had every servant round the table on her side, and they didn't even know the two women that Mary was talking about.

'As my old grandma used to say, God rest her soul,' Mary added with a deep sigh of affection. 'When you grow up, Mary, she said, it's not the ordinary plain-speaking people you have to be frightened of. Those you will know for what they are, and you will either like or dislike them as you please. No, says my grandma, it's the ones that are full of sweet-talk and smiles and empty promises that you have to watch. Those are the ones who will use you for their own gain and nothing more.'

'Yer old grandma told you true!' interrupted Mrs Ovens, pointing her spoon round the table and nodding in approval. 'My dear mother used to say near enough the same. Never trust anyone that comes to you dripping with smiles and sugar. As sure as Old Nick, they'll be nasty as acid if you put one foot wrong.'

'Smarmy gits, my ole dad used to call people like that,' said Joseph Bigg thoughtfully. 'Smarmy hypocrites that should be shot.'

Oh Lor'! thought Mrs Ovens with amused amazement. She's even got Joseph Bigg wanting to commit murder now!

'What did your mistress do to you, Mary?' asked a young parlour maid. 'You never did tell us what she done.'

Mary's eyes glittered like cold sapphires. 'She thought she could wipe me clean away as if I was no more important than a speck of dust on her table! Smash all my hopes and dreams as if they were no more valuable than cheap glass.'

'Oh, she sounds a nasty one, all right, this mistress of yorn!' said Mrs Ovens, dipping her bread into her stew and chuckling inwardly. 'So tell us what you done, Mary m'dear. Tell us how you wreaked your vengeance? And every little detail, mind!'

'Well,' said Mary, narrowing her eyes as she looked slowly round the table, 'I waited for her one dark night, when she thought I was long gone and herself forgotten by me. Foolish woman to think that I would ever forget *her*! I waited in the street just down from the house, and out she came ... walking as smug and as self-satisfied as ever you did see a person walking ... and then out of the darkness and quick as a flash I ran to her, and before anyone could see me – I stuck the knife in her! And down she flopped like a sack of flour. But not before she turned and looked me in the eyes, and saw – to her shocked surprise – who it was that had come out of the darkness and killed her.'

'Ohhhh!' Some of the maids were shuddering with delicious horror. It was awful and eerie and terrifying!

'It was justice!' Mary insisted, delicately dipping her spoon into her stew, while Mrs Ovens wiped the tears of laughter from her eyes with her apron. What a girl! What an imagination! And now came the big question that no one else had ever thought to ask Mary Neely. Now let's see how Mary would answer this one!

'So tell me, you little she-devil, if you did commit murder, how is it that the judge only gave you seven years in Botany Bay and not the noose? After all, that is the law, a life for a life.'

'Yeh, that's right!' said a maid. 'I got seven years for nicking a box of candles – so how come you got only the same for committing bloody murder?'

Mary's composure did not flicker. Mrs Ovens had to admire her. The sheer sauce of the girl was a treat to watch!

Mary finished her bread unhurriedly, smacked the crumbs delicately from her hands, then sat back languidly and surveyed her audience calmly.

'Life, I said to the judge, you may take my life in due exchange and I'll face my death bravely, because I do not repent of the deed, your worship. Nor will I ever repent! Not as long as I have breath. And the judge – a good man – he looks at me with the pitying and sorrowful eyes of a true Christian, and he says, "Miss Mary Neely, you have been cruelly wronged by that black-haired witch! And she did in all justice deserve to die. If it was up to me I would set you free, but the law is also cruel, and so I must punish you, with seven long years in Botany Bay."'

'Oh, ducky!' Mrs Ovens was laughing hysterically. 'It's a wonder that old judge didn't follow you out here himself ... Rachel, fetch my rum! I need it bad! And here was me pining for dear old London, but they don't get entertainment like this in Drury Lane!'

Tears spilled onto Mrs Ovens' fat cheeks. 'Mary, I got a soft spot for you, girl, because you got the manners of a lady and the tales of a scoundrel. Murder indeed!' Her whole body quaked with more laughter. She reached for her rum and gulped. 'Well, I tell you this, Mary Neely, you kill me!'

Chapter Twenty

Some days later, after a two-week excursion up country, George Jarvis met Mary Neely for the first time. He and Lachlan had just ridden up the drive to Government House, dismounted, and were handing their horses into the care of grooms when a curricle driven by Joseph Bigg came trotting up the path behind them.

Both men turned to look towards the open two-wheeled carriage where a girl was sitting with a baby in her arms.

'G'morning, sir,' Joseph Bigg touched his hat to the Governor. 'The boy was cranky an teethin' so Missis Macquarie asked us to take him out for a short ride in the cool air.'

'And now he is fast asleep,' Lachlan smiled, walking over to the carriage, opening the small door and reaching in to carefully lift his sleeping son from the girl's arms. 'May I?'

'Yes, sir.' The girl carefully handed the child over. 'He was asleep as soon as the curricle started moving,' she said.

Lachlan looked at the girl curiously. 'And you are?'

'Mary Neely, sir.'

Mary stepped down from the curricle and stood looking at the Governor with a nervous expression on her face. She was dressed in a neat blue dress and wore a straw bonnet over her golden hair.

'Are you the daughter of one of Elizabeth's friends?'

'No, sir.' Mary's cheeks flushed pink. 'I'm a convict-servant, sir.'

Lachlan was clearly surprised. The girl was obviously new to the household, and yet it was only the Chosen Few that Elizabeth allowed anywhere near their son. And Elizabeth was no fool when it came to judging character.

He said to the girl. 'Have you had much experience in looking after children?'

She shook her head. 'I've had none.'

'No experience? No younger brothers or sisters?'

'No, sir.'

Even more surprised by her direct truthfulness, Lachlan glanced at George to determine his reaction, but George's eyes were fixed on the girl.

And it was this unusual attention given by George Jarvis to the convict girl that made Lachlan look more keenly at her. He saw a pretty, light-haired girl with a slender shape and that was all.

'She's a good girl, Your Excellency.' Joseph Bigg had stepped down from his bench in order to speak up for the girl. 'And she has a knack with the baby there – soon as she lifts him up he stops cryin' – according to the mistress.'

'Then I am much obliged to you,' Lachlan said to the girl and turned away to carry his beloved son indoors.

Mary Neely and George Jarvis were left to follow, while Joseph Bigg climbed back on his bench to take the curricle and two horses back to the stables.

At the door to the house, George politely and silently stood aside to let the girl pass. And now they were only inches apart, she looked straight at George and he looked straight back at her.

'And you are George Jarvis,' she said.

'Yes, I know I am,' George answered.

She waited for him to say something more, not sure if he was being sarcastic, but when he didn't say anything more she was not sure whether to be amused or offended. She nodded briefly and walked on.

George watched her go. She moved with light and easy steps that made her look as if she might suddenly skip into a dance. Everything about her was too light and too lovely for her to harbour any dark secret, but this was New South Wales and she was a convict ... and knowing nothing about her yet, George's impulse to quicken his steps and catch up with her was checked by the thought that she might have committed some terrible crime.

Although, as he strolled slowly down the hall and watched her skip lightly up the stairs towards the nursery, his deep and powerful intuition told him that whatever her crime, it had to be something forgivable.

*

'What did she do?' George asked Lachlan.

It was the first time George Jarvis had ever

asked such a question about a convict.

Lachlan considered the papers on the table before him and decided to answer the question.

'Oh, nothing very bad. Elizabeth would not have allowed her near our child if she had.'

'But you checked her papers, nevertheless, as soon as you came in today?'

'Of course I did. Anyone who works close enough to get even a glimpse of my son is closely checked, as well you know.'

'So, what was her crime?'

'She was accused of stealing a small silver mirror from her mistress's bedroom. Her defence was that the maids in the attic had no mirror, but the mistress had many. So at night, especially when a maid had a night off, Miss Mary Neely would slip down to her mistress's bedroom and "borrow" a mirror. Until the night she was caught by a female guest, coming out of the bedroom of the lady of the house, carrying the mirror under her pinafore. Her mistress had her immediately arrested and charged at Leicester Assizes with theft, for which she was sentenced to seven years in Botany Bay.'

When George made no comment, Lachlan looked at him with smiling curiosity. 'So you've looked her over, have you, George? And now you want to know more about her?'

George shrugged. 'I was merely interested in her crime.'

'Well now you know. Her crime was the alleged theft of a small mirror. Elizabeth is quite certain that Mary Neely is basically a decent girl who would not hurt anyone.'

All this Mrs Ovens knew. Elizabeth had revealed Mary's true crime to her on the day the girl had been promoted upstairs and therefore entitled to eat in Mrs Ovens' kitchen.

Usually, the subject of a convict's crime was not something anyone asked or talked about. Whatever had happened was in the past and was their own business, and all they had left to do now was serve out their punishment and be done with it.

But it was time, Mrs Ovens decided, to end the fun and tell the truth to poor Mrs Kelly who had been suffering for weeks at the thought of having a murderess in their midst.

Mrs Kelly's black eyes nearly popped out of her head when Mrs Ovens told her over a glass of rum.

'It's the truth, m'deary, not a word of a lie. But why the girl has to keep saying she done murder is beyond me. I don't understand it at all.'

'Oh, well, now,' said Mrs Kelly, after a thoughtful pause. 'You don't understand because you've never been transported. It's a terrible thing. The voyage here on the convict ship is like a nightmare in hell. And the humiliation! Oh, that's the worst of all. Irons on your ankles. No water to wash the filth from your skin or clothes. The hatches battened down tight so there's no air, just the stinking stench of the crowded berths.'

'I don't bear to even imagine it,' said Mrs Ovens

pityingly.

Mrs Kelly nodded. 'And when life is that bad, when all hope seems gone, some people just lose their mind and go mad. But others – like our Mary – stay sane by thinking of the person that put them in that position, and that's when the fantasies of murder begin. In her mind Mary has probably killed that mistress of hers a thousand times and in a hundred different ways. And even now she is still fantasising. And sure she *knows* she is, but she feels free to do so because her former mistress is half a globe away and as safe as houses. But the fact that Mary needs the consolation of these fantasies shows the bitterness and hatred is still in her heart.'

'Then it's pitiable,' said Mrs Ovens, 'to let her heart burn up that way. But in time it will fade, surely?'

'Well now, that depends on how her life works out." Mrs Kelly sipped her rum and pressed her lips together. 'I know how Mary feels because I went through the same myself once upon a time, that I did. And this I know – if her life was to stay bad, then her craving for vengeance will get worse. But if it turns out not so bad, as mine has done, then the past *will* eventually fade away into forgetfulness.'

'She works the cards, you know? Works spells. Did she tell you? She uses the Black Queen to wreak evil on her former mistress.'

'So she said?' Mrs Kelly looked impressed. 'Now

I wonder who taught her that?'

Mrs Ovens poured herself some more rum. 'Speaking only for myself, and you know I'm not a vengeful person, Mrs Kelly, being brought up in a good Anglican-Church family as I was, but I hopes the Black Queen takes a ton of bad luck to that black-haired witch who consigned Mary to the bottom of a convict ship. Callous cow!'

*

The following morning Mary Neely met George Jarvis on the upstairs landing. Once again they both felt that instantaneous attraction of opposites, the fair to the dark, the dark to the fair, but there was something else, something more, and both felt it.

They regarded each other in silence but there was a subtle excitement in the sudden tensing of their bodies. Mary's face flushed the colour of roses.

'And you are Mary Neely,' he said.

Mary eyed him with amusement.

'Yes, I know I am,' she replied.

George smiled as she haughtily swept past him into the nursery.

*

In the days and weeks that followed George Jarvis and Mary Neely found it hard to keep away from each other, seeing as they both shared the same house, the same backstairs and front stairs, the same landings, and even on occasions the same private apartments of Governor and Mrs Macquarie.

Each day they waylaid each other on the upper landings or lower halls when their conversations grew longer and longer. Their meetings became tantalising interludes when time always seemed too short.

And then both, at the same time, developed a passionate love for quiet walks in the warm gardens of Government House between dinnertime and sunset, and both knew the path they were treading.

For George, just having Mary in the same world as himself gave a new and tender beauty to life, and nothing in nature could compare to the loveliness he saw in her face and those light blue eyes of hers. Whenever he saw her he felt his heart beating furiously, although he always faced her with a calm serenity that hid most of his thoughts and feelings.

For Mary, the influence of George's quiet and calm voice whenever he spoke seriously to her was beginning to dispel her melancholy and need for mysticism and creating spells of revenge. Everything he said to her seemed to fill her with a new sense of peace.

One morning he asked to see her pack of cards, and when she brought them to him, he instantly lifted out the Black Queen and tore it in two pieces before her shocked eyes.

'This is not the way,' he said quietly. 'In the East

we believe that "Heaven's way always comes around," and life eventually serves out its own justice.'

Mary stared at the two torn halves of the Queen of Spades and gave a shudder of superstitious terror.

'If you truly do believe in the power of the cards,' George said slowly, 'then you will know that *this* card always holds the power to break the spell of any black card in the pack.'

He handed her the Queen of Hearts.

The card of love.

She lifted her eyes and looked at him and felt the darkness leaving her soul. He had destroyed the Black Queen. The spell of the card and its hold on her thoughts was broken.

They stood facing each other in silence. Then a smile moved on her face as bright as the sun. She lifted the Queen of Hearts to her lips, kissed it, and handed the card back to him.

A new spell had begun.

Chapter Twenty-One

The ship, the *General Browne*, finally arrived in Sydney Harbour carrying two hundred and fifty tons of Bengal grain.

As relieved as he was, Lachlan was livid when he saw its inferior quality. 'They would never dare to send this *dirt* to England!'

Even more galling was the fact that a third of the weight of the Bengal grain consisted of the weevils swarming through it.

The sifting process began. And while it did, Lachlan realised that his threats against those settlers hoarding hidden grain would now be laughed at. Even the convicts objected to eating Indian weevils.

As the months passed the situation became even worse: the hot summer sun of January and February had burned every new shoot of grass. Bush fires began to rage. By March 1815 more than five thousand cattle and three thousand sheep had died.

Lachlan silently looked towards Heaven for help ... and as he did so, his eyes rested on the Blue Mountains.

*

The Blue Mountains, which hemmed in New South Wales from the rest of the continent, truly were blue. Maybe it was the reflection of the blue sea and the blue sky that coloured the mist that hung over them.

The mountains were covered in density with huge trees and thick bush. Speculators in the past had been sure that rich verdure and shaded grazing land lay beyond the Blue Mountains, breaking their way through briar and bush, but those explorers had returned after travelling miles, unable to go any further forward due to the rocks and granite boulders that were impossible to pass.

'Some say China lies beyond,' said George Evans, the emancipist engineer and surveyor.

'I have been to China,' Lachlan said, 'and so I know it is *not* behind those mountains.'

Still, in the days and weeks that followed, Lachlan could think of nothing else but the Blue Mountains and the possibilities that may lie beyond them. He studied every report from every previous explorer, from Flinders to Blaxland, and all their observations led him to believe that the only possible way over the Blue Mountains – if there was a way – was in the west.

He decided to visit King Bungeree, certain there were Aboriginal trails all over those mountains. After all, this had been *their* land for aeons, before the white men had come and taken it from them.

*

Normally King Bungaree would never discuss the exploration to find more land with any white man, but to the Aboriginals and King Bungeree, '*Massa*

Mawarrie' was more than just a white man – he was a *King-Man* who strode over this land of *Koori* like a colossus of greatness, a *King-Man* of brightness and goodness who used only kind words and kind gifts – not a despot of discrimination and prejudice who ruled *Koori* with no other command but the lash of the whip.

So, after sharing the refreshment of some fruit together, King Bungeree confessed to Lachlan there was a wonderful land beyond the Blue Mountains, a place far, far beyond where other Aboriginal peoples had lived from the beginning of time and still lived there – a place called *'uluru'* – but his own people, no, they had only ever lived in *Koori*.

Lachlan knew that *Koori* was and had always been the Aboriginal name for the land that the British now called New South Wales, but *uluru* – King Bungeree spoke of it with a reverence of tone and wonder that a white man might speak of the mythical *'Shangrila'*.

So did it even exist ... or was it some place of ancestral Aboriginal folklore that existed only in King Bungeree's imagination?

'It is not only from our *Dreamings'*, King Bungeree said, as if reading Lachlan's thoughts. 'Aboriginal peoples have been crossing the Blue Mountains for thousands of years before the white men came.'

Lachlan was stunned. 'You mean ... you know the way across?'

King Bungeree nodded. 'We know our *own* way across.'

'Will you tell me that way?'

King Bungeree thought for a while, and then sighed and said slowly, 'The white men came and found *Koori* with no help from us ... The white men invaded our land with no agreement from us. So why now do the white men not go and find a way to cross the Blue Mountains ... with no help from us.'

Lachlan understood, and because he understood he had always felt sympathy for the Aboriginal people, but he had been commissioned and given a job to do in the name of his own King, and it was his duty to do that job in the best way he could.

He sat for a long reflective moment thinking of Blaxland, Lawson and Wentworth, three white men who *had* found a way into and across a small part of the Blue Mountains, but only for a distance of fifty-six miles and it had achieved them little, leading to their return.

And now – even those three men still did not know what lay *beyond* the Blue Mountains.

He said quietly to King Bungeree. 'The white men *will* find a way across the Blue Mountains to whatever is beyond. If not now, then in some future time. But now it is essential to the people's health and existence here that they do find a way across the Blue Mountains, if only for the purpose of finding more land to grow more food. And I came to you, King Bungaree, because I had hoped the Aboriginal people would help us.'

King Bungaree sat staring at the sky and refused to answer.

'Not even some hint?' Lachlan asked. 'Not even, perhaps, a finger pointing in the right direction?

King Bungeree turned his head and looked silently at Lachlan for a long time.

'You are good white man, Massa Mawarrie, good friend to Bungaree and his people,' he said finally, and then he slowly raised his hand, pointing west.

*

A few days later Lachlan sent George Evans and a small party on an expedition of discovery. He made their object clear.

'If possible, the discovery of some new tract of country fit for agricultural cultivation that might help us to grow more food to feed the colony and not have to rely and wait on ships from other countries.'

George Evans nodded, marking his map. 'From Sydney – the westward route.'

Lachlan saw the explorers off on their journey, having agreed that they could take with them an Irish guide named Tom Byrne who was excellent at shooting kangaroos, a handy skill if food was desperately needed. James Coogan, John Grover and John Tighe, all ex-convicts, accompanied them. Their orders were to venture as far as they pssibly could, so Lachlan knew it was going to be a long wait for their return.

Meanwhile, from the place that he now called,

'*our Newcastle*', he sold one hundred and fifty tons of coal to Calcutta, to be repaid in Bengal grain which he gave to the convicts, more and more of whom needed to be fed by the Government. The drought had ruined many of the small emancipist farmers who found they had no means of business, and were left with no choice but to give their assigned convict labourers and servants back to the Government, no longer able to meet the cost of feeding them.

The drought continued, without a sign of rain.

The *Betsy* finally arrived from India with another two hundred and fifty tons of life-saving grain, with a smaller proportion of weevils.

*

Two months later, George Evans and his party returned from their expedition of discovery and reported their findings to the Governor. This time it was certain they *had* crossed the Blue Mountains and seen beyond them.

'We rested on the bank of a running river,' Evans said excitedly. And we saw meadowlands clear of trees, and good soil watered by chains of waterholes not affected by the drought. It rained, and drenched us to the skin.'

'Rained!'

'Only for a day, but rain it was!' said Evans. And his report went on, just as he and his party of explorers had done, further and further into the unknown.

He described the lovely scenes they had seen: green grass which looked so good after the burned-out territory they had left behind – *'Grass so abundant and fresh – and so high we had to wade our way through it,'* Evans said excitedly.

They had crossed the mountain boundaries that marked the eastern and western watershed of the region. That was why they had tasted rain when Sydney had not.

From the Blue Mountains they had seen open country stretching as far as the eyes could see, with a long river flowing through it. Although, Evans added, in his opinion this long river could not in any way be reached from the eastern range without difficulty, and as the mountains there were covered with granite it would be difficult to push a horse faster than a walk.

'But the land to the west that we saw,' Evans continued elatedly, 'I cannot speak too highly of it or describe to you what beautiful country it is – rich enough and big enough to grow food and raise cattle and sheep on it for more than a hundred years!'

Lachlan could hardly believe it or restrain his own excitement – Evans and his team had travelled one hundred and fifty miles and seen a beautiful country of huge extent and great fertility – *Shangrila!*

'Did you mark out the route?' he asked.

'Oh yes,' Evans laughed, 'we marked the route on our maps as we went along. Too right we did!'

191

And they had indeed! As Lachlan studied their maps he realised that they had found the elusive large river that the explorer, Captain Matthew Flinders, had spent so long searching for.

Flinders had been convinced that a large river was there, somewhere, but he and his explorers had searched for miles along the coast looking for a start to the river from the sea. It had never occurred to Flinders that the river was inland – a *freshwater* river – beyond the Blue Mountains.

And so Lachlan Macquarie – the same man who, as a young officer in India, had once organised the building of a road over the treacherous Indian mountain Ghauts into the land of Mysore, now began to draw up his own specifications for the building of a road climbing more than four thousand feet and one hundred and fifty miles long, based on Evan's westward route, across the Blue Mountains, into the new Australia.

And in that new land to the west, George Evans was to be rewarded with a grant of one thousand acres of land sealed to his name, and the same grant of one thousand acres was also to be given and sealed to the names of Tom Byrne and the other three ex-convicts who had travelled with Evans

Inside Government House, Lachlan invited George Evans and his four explorers to raise their glasses and drink a toast with him.

'Gentlemen – from here into the new and bigger Australia.'

'*Aussssstralliiaaa!*' the four ex-convicts cheered, while the Governor and George Evans laughed.

Chapter Twenty-Two

Less than a month had passed since his return, and George Evans was once again preparing for another expedition into the mountains, joined by a huge number of people this time, because a road was going to be built along the way.

'The road must be at least twelve feet wide,' Lachlan instructed William Cox, a former member of New South Wales Corps who lived in Windsor and was joining the expedition.

'Why twelve feet?' Cox asked.

'Because when the road is completed, homes will need to be built if farmers are to live and work the land there, so building materials will have to be transported up the road, and depots will have to established, food and timber carried up, so the road will need to be wide enough to allow two carts to pass each other with ease and without any danger or difficulty.'

'The expense of such a road,' Lachlan wrote in explanation to the Colonial Secretary, Lord Bathurst, *'would be trifling, as I have offered the convicts who will be doing all the hard labour the reward of receiving their ticket-of-leave and emancipation on completion of the road.*

It was a masterstroke – the greatest incentive that could have been offered to any convict. The hard slog of cutting through bush and briar and building a road of four thousand feet up and across the mountains under tough and rough conditions would not be a punishment, nor would there be a chance of escape because a guard of soldiers would go with them – but every step the convicts took would be a step further on their path to freedom. That would be their goal and their reward at the end of the road: Governor Macquarie's certificate of emancipation.

As the huge expedition set off to leave, the Governor gave the convicts some final few words of encouragement.

'No whip at your back and a great achievement ahead of you – not only for each of you personally, but for all the people of Australia.'

And just in case Lord Bathurst objected, Lachlan forestalled any opposition with an outrageous piece of flattery that no Minister at the Colonial Office would be able to resist – the site of the first town he planned to be built on the route of the road, would be named *Bathurst*, adding:

'For many of the convicts it will knock only a year or so off their sentences, and this way the work needed will be done with greater effort and with less trouble.'

Upon receipt of the letter Lord Bathurst was delighted that his family name would be immortalised in a new land on the other side of world – but the Exclusives saw it as just one more example of Macquarie's infamy – selling freedom to convicts.

*

The drought continued relentlessly on the eastern side of the mountains. In the region of Sydney and its outlands the rivers had dried up. The Government Stores had almost run out of grain.

In the town of Sydney the merchants were selling wheat at £2 a bushel. These speculators had held out until the price was as high as it could go, and now they were making a small fortune!

Every complaint was taken to the Governor, the people clamouring to give him their tales of woe and deprivation. Wheat at £2 a bushel was completely beyond them. Soon they would have no bread at all to give to their children. Could he not force the Exclusives to reduce the price?

No, he could not. They were *free* settlers – free to do whatever they liked. He could only threaten them with empty threats. Then he sent for more cheap wheat from Bengal.

And while he waited for its arrival, and in order to feed all the soldiers and convicts, he was finally forced to use large amounts of Government money to buy the local wheat from the Exclusives at £2 a bushel.

In October 1815, after a disastrous three-year drought, the rains at last fell as heavily as an Indian monsoon over New South Wales.

Chapter Twenty-Three

In 1816, Lachlan Macquarie made history by becoming the longest-serving Governor of New South Wales.

The two years he had agreed to stay had turned into six years, and still he showed no signs of wishing to return home, telling Elizabeth – 'There's too much work still to be done here.'

The new Foreign Secretary, Lord Castlereagh, sent him a dispatch stating, '*Lord Bathurst tells us you have served us very well ...*' then Castlereagh went on to offer Lachlan, upon his return to England, a pension for life of £1000 a year in return for his service in the Colony – if he would continue ruling the Colony and agree to stay for a further two years.

Lachlan replied:

The Colony, as you call it, is now developing beyond its former state of a small convict settlement into a country we have named Australia.

The Blue Mountains have been crossed and the area of land has expanded into the interior where regular towns and new habitations are already under construction.

Numerous Georgian-style buildings have also been built in the town of Sydney itself, as well as two schools and two churches and a home for orphaned children, all designed by the skill of emancipist architects and surveyors and erected by the labour of the convicts.

'I don't know about a measly pension,' Elizabeth said curtly. 'It's a knighthood they should be offering you.'

Chapter Twenty-Four

Mary Neely no longer cared about where she was or what had happened to her on the transport ship or anywhere else before arriving in New South Wales, all she knew was that her life now in Government House was wonderful, because George Jarvis was there.

George was the handsomest man she had ever seen, so full of that strange attractive charm that was his alone. Even his conversations with her were different to any others she had heard or known.

The gardens of Government House now bloomed with roses and many other beautiful botanical varieties, all due to the passionate work of Mrs Macquarie who had now introduced some tame wallabies to languish or play on the front lawns.

But it was the long and large gardens at the back of the house, filled with large bushes and private little pathways where Mary often met George to take an evening walk, away from the prying eyes of others in the household.

During one of their walks George stopped by a bush of beautiful red roses, plucked one, and handed it to her.

Mary held the rose in her hands and smelled its delicate perfume.

'I have always loved English roses,' she said.

'Roses are not an English flower, Mary, all roses originate in the East.'

She looked into his face and protested, 'That can't be true. Everyone knows that roses come from England.'

'No, travellers have carried the seeds back to England and elsewhere, but the roses that grow all over the world have all descended from the Persian rose.'

Mary looked amazed, she had not known that, and how could she know, until now.

'I thought ... we all thought ... that roses were an English flower.'

George sighed and said softly. 'Yes, that is the delusion of many.'

Everything George said to Mary after that was like poetry to her ears. Some of the time it was in fact poetry, for his love of the Persian poets was still passionate.

Her own knowledge of poems was more limited than his, but as they shared their walks in the garden, she shared what poetry she knew with him. He found he could not relate to her English poetry, it was too whimsical for him. In contemplation of life, he preferred instead the realism of Omar Khayaam.

'This world will long survive our poor departure,
Persisting without name or note of us.
Before we came, it never begrudged our absence;
When we have gone, how can it feel regret?'

The poem vexed and saddened Mary. How could this man Khayaam have such a cheerless view of the world? How could anyone enjoy his words when they made a person feel so unimportant? What had made him such a sad old Persian?

George laughed. 'Khayaam was never *sad*. He believed in the Creator and Heaven and Destiny, but most of all he believed in the wonderful gift of *life* itself. Of living and enjoying *life* itself while we have it. Who else but a man who truly loved life would write,

> Allow no shadow of regret to cloud you,
> No unnecessary grief to overcast your days.
> Never renounce laughter or love songs
> Until your bones lay mixed with elder clay.'

Mary still did not like it, the poetry of this Khayaam, but it helped her to understand the thoughts and attitude that led George to remain so calm and steady amidst the turbulence of life.

Her thoughts had stopped her, but George had wandered slowly on down one of the long darkening paths in a contemplative mood, pausing to stand and look up at the sky with a sudden smile on his face.

'George?'

At the sound of his name he turned and slowly walked back towards her.

'What were you smiling at?'

'I was smiling at myself, Mary.'

'What for?'

'For thinking that anyone who lived before us could tell us how to live now ... in a different world and a different time ... my own foolishness.'

She looked at the amusement in his dark eyes, and felt the strength and sense leaving her. She had a sudden longing, here alone with him in the quietness of the garden, to slip her arms around his waist and press her mouth to his and kiss him with passion, a deep intense passion that had began to fill her mind and heart and make her pulses spring alive every time she saw him.

'Ello darlin.'

The voice broke her trance and she jumped and turned. George laughed as he looked over at a branch where a white cockatoo was looking at them sideways.

'Bappoo ...' He moved over to the branch and the parrot climbed onto his arm. 'Hello, Bappoo.'

'Ello darlin.'

'Why do you call him Bappoo?' Mary asked.

'I named him after our House Steward in India,' George replied, 'because whenever he spoke, Bappoo also liked to imitate the way Englishmen speak.'

And when George began to tell her about Bappoo, a huge lovable man in his turban and voluminous pantaloons, Mary thought she would die laughing as George imitated the way Bappoo spoke – *Yes, my dear, by God, by Jove, I report you to Lachlan-Sahib because you bad boy, naughty naughty ... you rascally son of slave!'*

When Mary had stopped laughing she was curious about the word 'slave'.

'Did Governor Macquarie have slaves in his house in India?'

'No.' George had seen Mr Byrne, the head gardener, coming down the path.

He walked towards him and held out his own arm to allow Mr Byrne to take the cockatoo and receive the bird's usual greeting. *'Ello darlin.'*

'I'll *darlin* him, if he gets out of his cage again,' Mr Byrne grunted.

George frowned. 'You keep him in a cage?'

'Only at night, Mr Jarvis, only at night. Mrs Macquarie won't have him disturbing the sleep of her wallabies out front, so she won't.'

'And how could little Bappoo disturb them?' George asked mildly.

'With his non-stop *"ello darlin"* – drives me mad sometimes he does.'

'Then teach him to say something else,' George suggested. 'If he can learn two words, he can learn more.'

The gardener puckered his lips for a moment. 'Missus Macquarie don't like him talking at all, she says it's unnatural.'

'Then teach him to say just that.'

'How d'ye mean?'

George imitated the parrot's voice. *'Ello darlin – oh, this is unnatural! Ello darlin – oh yes my dear, by God, by Jove – this talking of mine is unnatural!'*

Even the bird was squawking and flapping when George had finished, unsettled by the laughter of Mr Byrne and Mary.

*

'There's nothing between you and George is there?' asked Mrs Ovens secretively when she got a moment alone with the girl the following morning.

'Nothing, Mrs Ovens, nothing at all ...' Mary was straining halfway out the window on the front landing, eagerly watching George Jarvis, looking so handsome, wearing riding breeches and leggings of brown leather and a cool white shirt, riding down the driveway beside Governor Macquarie.

When she withdrew and turned round to face Mrs Ovens, her blue eyes were sparkling. 'Where on earth did you get such a ridiculous notion?'

Mrs Ovens rocked with laughter as she told Mrs Kelly later that night. 'She likes him, likes him a lot, she does. And he likes her too.'

Mrs Kelly's eyes became dark with memories, and then she endowed the air with one of her huge sighs.

'Ah, he's only playing with her. She shouldn't trust him. Trust no man is my motto. If she gives in to him, he will only use her as his plaything. Then when he's got her where he wants, lying on her back, with her hair like a cloud on his pillow, he'll use her lovely young body only for his enjoyment, only for his own selfish pleasure, and then he'll deceive her...'

Mrs Kelly quivered emotionally, sat back in her chair and put a hand to her brow in grief. 'As I myself was used, and deceived...'

Mrs Ovens shuddered deliciously and rushed for the rum; she loved to hear the stories of Mrs Kelly and her lover in Ireland, a handsome young rogue who had seduced her into a whole springtime of passionate lovemaking, and then had deceived her shamelessly – and she a defenceless young widow – unjustly sent to Botany Bay for near killing him.

'But the *romance*, m'dear,' said Mrs Ovens as she pressed a glass of rum into Mrs Kelly's hand. 'And the thrill you felt that first day he touched you ... As you often say, it does no harm to turn the memory back to the good times.'

'Oh!' sighed Mrs Kelly passionately. 'Will I ever forget?'

Mrs Ovens sipped her rum excitedly, moistened her lips, and urged Mrs Kelly to tell of her lover.

Mrs Kelly again sighed deeply. 'Young I was then, young and tender. As slim as a larch, with the hair rippling like a fountain of black silk down my back, and my skin as smooth as pure milk. And he – he the fair and handsome son of the squire; charming, elegant, and so respectable you would think butter wouldn't melt in his mouth.

'A young widow I was when he calls on me in my cottage. And then he stretches out a hand to caress my skirt as I served him a glass of ale. I was so shocked I just *looked* at his hand caressing my skirt ... then I looked at his smile. Oh! What a smile! And there I stood with suspended breath, my heart quivering, drawn between desire and pride. I looked into his shining eyes until my breast just rose in confusion.

'"If you are not sure," he says to me later, "then draw back, draw back now my darling," he says, holding me so tight against him I could hardly breathe. "For, oh, my love, I do not want to press you against your will," he says, as I was laid down with misgivings...'

An hour later Mrs Ovens lifted her apron and wiped the tears from her eyes. 'Such a rascally young man, but *what* a lover!'

'Aye, after that first time, he only had to reach out and I was his for the taking.' Mrs Kelly's bosom heaved in another turbulent sigh that convulsed her body, and then she collapsed back in her chair like a spent storm.

'So you see,' she said, recovering herself, 'Mary must be warned in time. No man is to be trusted until he puts a wedding band on. And even then he must be watched with a suspicious eye.'

The next morning Mary listened silently as Mrs Kelly sought to warn her. 'I am only trying to spare you the heartbreak that fell to me, cherub. Have nothing to do with him!'

And later, Mrs Ovens advised her in a totally different way, quite the opposite. 'I knows George, and I knows he's fine and decent, so if you can have a bit of a romance with him then do so while you can, because I warn you, Mary, that's all you'll get – a bit of harmless romance – because Governor Macquarie would never allow George to get too serious about any convict girl.'

But Mary would not be warned, and only minutes later when she made her escape and ran like lightning up the grand staircase and turned onto the landing – she crashed straight into George Jarvis. His arms instinctively caught her before she slipped, holding her close for a moment, and they smiled into each other's eyes.

'*Saints above!*' cried Mrs Kelly.

Mary whirled round to see the Irish cook standing there with a tray in her hands.

'No good will come of it!' said Mrs Kelly. 'And you, George Jarvis, you should be ashamed of yourself, taking advantage of a poor servant girl that's not wise to men.'

'Mrs Kelly!' Mary gasped, mortified. 'George just saved me from tripping over, that's all.'

And he has never taken advantage of me, never even kissed me, Mary wanted to shout at the cook, *and he probably never will now because of you!*

Mrs Kelly lifted her chin haughtily. 'Now, you, Mary, come along or I shall tell Governor Macquarie about your loose behaviour. And that will be *you* back in the kitchen washing dishes and cleaning floors and no more being nursemaid, won't it?'

Mary was so embarrassed she could not have looked at George to save her life.

'Mrs Kelly,' George said calmly, 'there is no need

for you to try and frighten Mary with threats of reports to the Governor.'

'The Governor don't like no finagling between the sexes in his house, boyo! That he don't!'

'He doesn't like any rum drinking in the kitchen either,' George said. 'I clearly remember him forbidding it. Do you remember also?'

Mary looked at George now – just the threat of depriving Mrs Kelly and Mrs Ovens of their nightly rum would be as bad as taking their breath away.

Mrs Kelly stared at him dumbly as if she had forgotten what she intended to say next.

George rolled his hand down in an exaggerated salaam to Mrs Kelly, smiled at Mary, and then turned and strolled away.

'Oh now,' said Mrs Kelly, watching him go with narrowed eyes. 'Now there's a one to watch!' She looked at Mary warningly. 'Have nothing to do with him, Mary. He's only a man, and men only like to amuse themselves. No rum in the kitchen indeed!'

She left Mary abruptly with shoes tattooing rapidly along the landing as if she couldn't wait to deposit her tray and get back to tell Mrs Ovens.

'Ah, George Jarvis would never tell,' said Mrs Ovens carelessly. 'You forget, Mrs Kelly m'dear, that I knows George better than you do. I came out here in the same ship as him.'

Mrs Kelly did not answer immediately, her eyes fixed on some distant memory. 'He was holding her as tight as tight can be ... God knows what else he would have done to her if I hadn't come along in the nick of time.'

'Dear! Dear!' Mrs Ovens could think of nothing more exciting than a new young romance to liven the talk downstairs. She wished Mrs Kelly would leave matters be. All was grist to the mill and provided enjoyable breaks in the monotony of the kitchen, and never a dull moment lately, not since Mary arrived. She was such a lovey, such fun with the other girls, and such a beauty – that's why that mistress of hers in England had jumped on the excuse of the "theft" of a small mirror to get rid of her. Mrs Ovens was certain of it.

'They live in the same house and so you can't prevent them meeting,' Mrs Ovens protested. 'And so what if she does have a fancy for George Jarvis? What's wrong with that?'

'Oh, he's much worse than other men, that George Jarvis,' Mrs Kelly insisted. 'Not fit in any way to beguile any innocent young girl. Don't you know that in the country where he comes from, the men are so lusty they don't even bother deceiving a woman, they just go to bed with two or three women at the same time. Aye – *harems* – they call them!' Mrs Kelly's head nodded insistently. 'Aye, that's how the men carry on in that land where George Jarvis comes from. Mary must be warned!'

Mrs Ovens tutted, 'I don't think Mary would care if you told her that George came from the moon or Mars or some place even stranger than that. Now why do you have to go and spoil things? Are you forgetting, m'ducky, that you were once young and in love yourself?'

'Ohhhh!' cried Mrs Kelly passionately, flopping back in her chair and putting a hand to her brow. 'Will I ever forget! And me just an innocent young widow ...'

'That's more like it,' smiled Mrs Ovens, settling herself more comfortably in her chair in readiness to hear more about Mrs Kelly's handsome young lover.

'Tell me in what way you almost killed the rascal and got charged with attempted murder?'

Chapter Twenty-Five

In London, John McArthur knew his time to move against Lachlan Macquarie had come.

Being one of the masterminds behind the coup against Governor Bligh, and having travelled to London to defend himself against all charges, John McArthur had got off lightly, but as the Colonial Office regarded him as one of the main troublemakers in that shameful affair, it had steadfastly refused to allow McArthur to return to New South Wales – despite the fact that before leaving the Colony he had secured himself a vast landholding near the Hawkesbury River, as well as a huge number of sheep.

Over the years John McArthur's place in New South Wales had grown into a rich man's plantation in both size and grandeur, which for the past eight years had been run by his wife, Elizabeth, who had remained behind.

But she would not be running it on her own for much longer, McArthur was determined, and the large number of assigned convicts who were helping her to run it would soon find their days of ease and Macquarie's 'Sundays free from work' to be a thing of the past.

Even now, John McArthur could not believe that Governor Macquarie had officially banned all flogging of assigned convicts by their masters, unless a crime had been committed and an order

211

was for any flogging was to be given by a magistrate.

The changes that were continually taking place in New South Wales appalled John McArthur, but there was one change – the worst of all – that utterly sickened him.

'*Can it really be true,*' he wrote with disgust in a letter to his wife, '*that Governor Macquarie has invited men who once wore leg-irons to dine at his table in Government House?*'

Proving that during his years in exile in England, McArthur had kept in constant touch with those Exclusives who held the same view as he did regarding emancipists.

*

In the Colonial Office, Lord Bathurst had a reputation of being '*a very busy man*' and indeed he was. It was in Bathurst's nature to keep himself busy at all times, whether he needed to or not, and sometimes the strain became too much for him.

In response to the endless letters of complaints he had been receiving for years about Governor Macquarie from the Exclusives in the Colony, he finally wrote a letter to the Governor warning him to be less helpful to the emancipists, to implement harsher rules and greater punishments for the convicts, and – most importantly – to give as much support and patronage as possible to the free settlers who were, naturally, more deserving than the emancipists, and who had sent him many complaints about the Governor's liberal attitude and leniencies.

*

So now that the Colonial Office was seeking to reprimand and oppose him, and take the side of that sanctimonious elitist group which Elizabeth had began to refer to lately as *"those villains"* because of their obsession in trying to cause trouble for him at every turn, Lachlan replied to Lord Bathurst and, with undisguised contempt, gave his own view on the situation:

> *'No doubt, many of the free settlers (if not all) would prefer never to admit any persons who had been convicts to any situation of equality with themselves. But in my humble opinion, in coming to New South Wales they should consider that they are coming to a convict country, and if they are too proud or too delicate in their feelings to associate with the population of this country, then they should bend their course to some other country in which their prejudices in this respect would meet with no opposition.'*

Then he defended his principle of appointing emancipists to positions of civic office.

> *'My principle is, that when once a man is free, his former state should no longer be*

remembered, or allowed to act against him. What can be so great a stimulus to a man of respectable family and education, who has fallen to the lowest state of degradation, as to know, that it is still in his power to recover what he has lost, and not only to become a worthy member of society, but to be treated as such? Let punishment be as severe as may be necessary, but when that which the Law has ordained has been fulfilled, for the sake of mercy and justice - there let it terminate.'

But he was becoming sick of all the complaints and petty tirades of the Exclusives, he had done his eight years, and he had done his best, so in the same dispatch with his reply to the Earl of Bathurst, Lachlan tended his resignation to both the Colonial Office and the King.

Chapter Twenty-Six

In the meantime, while he waited for a response, Lachlan Macquarie's plans for the new Australia continued.

He had brought the colony through two famines, had overseen the building of roads across the Blue Mountains, and despite the financial restrictions imposed on him by the Treasury officials in London, who could not understand his enthusiasm for erecting fine architecture in a convict colony, he continued to administer New South Wales with humanity and courage, and an unswerving belief in its future.

On 8th April 1817, in Sydney, the doors of the first *Bank of New South Wales* were opened with great ceremony.

It was to prove a life-saver to many of the settlers who did not want to leave the land on which they had built their houses, and applied to the Bank for a mortgage instead, agreeing to pay back the loan with interest as the climate and times improved.

Governor Macquarie was very proud of the new bank. He firmly believed it would save the Colony from eventual ruin, and said so many times during long meetings over dinner with prospective shareholders at Government House.

A board of Directors had been appointed, with George Howe of the *Gazette* becoming one of the shareholders. Happy was delighted with his new position. He had handed over the editorship of the *Gazette* to his twenty-year-old son, Robert Howe.

On the day the first *Bank of New South Wales* officially opened for business, after a number of speeches from the directors, the first depositor, Sergeant Murphy of the 73rd Regiment marched up to the cashier and deposited the colossal sum of £50.

The directors were beaming: even the military were prepared to trust the new bank.

Their smiles quickly vanished when the second depositor proudly marched in – a male convict servant, not yet freed, who became very indignant when his *promissory note* was not accepted as a cash deposit.

*

In London, in the Colonial Office, Lord Bathurst was once again '*very busy*' writing a reply to Governor Macquarie, a man to whom he had always given his unfailing support, assuring the Governor that his previous letter did not in any way imply a lack of faith in him, and as a consequence he was refusing to pass on his resignation to the King.

> '... I cannot give a better proof of the confidence which is still reposed in you, than by deciding not to take any measure for appointing a successor to you, unless I shall learn that you persist in your determination

to return to England.'

Before Bathurst could arrange for the dispatch of the letter, he received yet another visit from John McArthur.

This time, McArthur informed Lord Bathurst that he had secured the support of some of the most influential people in London for his application to return to New South Wales, and one of those influential gentlemen was Sir Thomas Brisbane.

Chapter Twenty-Seven

'Brisbane?'

Lord Bathhurst and the Colonial Office had always held firm in their refusals to allow John McArthur to return to New South Wales, but if a growing number of men of rank and class in England were now supporting him ...

'Our main concern is for Governor Macquarie,' said Bathurst sternly. 'We cannot risk another coup against the King's Viceroy in the Antipodes like that carried out against Governor Bligh – and *you,* Mr McArthur, were one of the main manipulators behind that coup.'

'For which I have apologised many times,' McArthur replied with a fake sincerity. 'And had I known those officers of the New South Wales Corps were planning a revolt against Governor Bligh, I would have had nothing at all to do with them.'

Lord Bathurst's face remained stern as he listened to John McArthur, still unsure whether to believe him ... but if men of rank and class were supporting him ...

'And Governor Macquarie is, I am told, a very different type of ruler than Governor Bligh,' John McArthur added. 'They say he is a humane man, of great energy and intellect, as well as possessing a very courteous and gentlemanly manner.'

'That is correct.'

'So who in New South Wales could possibly wish to oppose him? Not I, certainly. Nor would I wish to tie my horse to the wagons of any others who would wish to oppose him.'

When Lord Bathurst remained silent, his eyes still cold, John McArthur insisted, 'I assure you, my lord, I have only one interest in life, and that is sheep.'

Lord Bathurst finally blinked. 'Sheep?'

'Yes, my lord, the flocks of sheep I already own and hope to extend in New South Wales.'

And then John McArthur pressed on, telling Lord Bathurst the same things he had told all the other men of the ruling class in England who now supported him ... that now the Blue Mountains had been crossed and fine grazing land had been found on the other side, the new wealth of the Colony could be created from the rearing of sheep, huge herds of them, making the Colony self-sufficient in its own right without having to depend on all of its bills being met by England.

Lord Bathurst sat thoughtful, realising how valuable the supply of cheap Australian wool would be for the Mills in England, much less expensive than foreign imports.

He said, 'The land in New South Wales is British land, so any wool exported from there would in fact be *British* wool, and therefore it would have to be supplied to us at a very reasonable cost by the sheep farmers.'

John McArthur forced a smile. 'Certainly, my

lord, it will be the cheapest wool in the world.'

And seeing Bathurst's awakening interest, John McArthur took that opportunity to fire the same sly salvo against Lachlan Macquarie that he had subtly done with those other Englishmen of wealth and rank.

'And with the Colony eventually being able to support itself from the sale of wool from its own sheep,' McArthur added, 'Governor Macquarie could still have his buildings of the finest architecture in his city of convicts without the cost being met by the Colonial Office.'

'Finest architecture?' Lord Bathurst frowned. 'My understanding is that all buildings have been ones of absolute necessity, such as schools and a hospital and a church.'

'Just so, just so,' McArthur agreed, 'and I believe they are very impressive and grand with no expense spared in their construction. A home for orphans too, and even a village and a school for the Aborigines! And there. my lord, is the difference between Governor Bligh and Governor Macquarie...' John McArthur sighed admirably. 'Governor Bligh would *never* have been so kind to the Aborigines by using money sent from the Colonial Office, but Governor Macquarie ... England must be very proud of him.'

The chilled expression on Lord Bathurst's face still had John McArthur smiling a week later when, with official permission finally granted, he set off to board his ship back to his wife and his family and New South Wales.

What a fool Bathurst was, and how easily the English ruling pomps were seduced by their own greed, McArthur was thinking as his ship set sail.

'If it came in plenty, we could even sell some of that wool to other countries in Europe,' Sir Thomas Brisbane had said excitedly. *'Wool is a very valuable commodity there too.'*

But what neither Brisbane nor Bathurst nor any of those other high-ranking gentlemen knew, was that he, John McArthur, held the monopoly in New South Wales of pure merino rams that would be so necessary for the breeding of more sheep, and the growth and production of so much wool.

Oh, yes, indeed. England could well make a huge fortune in the future from the cheap wool sent to them from New South Wales – but not before John McArthur had made his own huge fortune first.

PART FOUR

Chapter Twenty-Eight

It was now over eight months since John McArthur had left England to return to New South Wales; and Lord Bathurst was still being inundated with letters from the colony's Exclusive faction who continued to dip their pens in bitter gall to send him their relentless complaints about Governor Macquarie.

Although now it was not only to the Colonial Office they were sending their infuriated letters, but also to influential people of the ruling class as well as to Members of Parliament.

England was almost bankrupt due to the cost of its long war with France; the poor were even poorer, and even the rich were finding it hard to stay rich. The crime rate continued to rise, and threats of a *'people's revolt'* to bring down the government were escalating.

The shadows of the French Revolution still darkened the corridors of Whitehall and Westminster and those Members of Parliament who were constantly being heckled in the House of Commons and threatened by their constituents on the street, were now using the letters from the Exclusives to save themselves from all accusations of incompetence.

In Lachlan Macquarie – the Exclusives had gifted these politicians with the perfect scapegoat to detract attention and blame from themselves.

And as the man himself was twelve thousand miles and half the globe away, how could he refute any of it?

Their first public accusation against the Governor of New South Wales was the horrendous *financial cost* to the United Kingdom for his building programmes.

'It seems...' one politician declared, 'that convicts transported to the antipodes no longer find themselves arriving in a *penal colony* – but in a place to rival *one of Europe's finest cities!*'

They even charged him with being responsible for Britain's rising crime, insisting that many of those soldiers who had limped home from the blood-soaked battlefield of Waterloo, and with no other employment available to them, had consequently and deliberately gone out to commit crime in the hope of being transported to Macquarie's promised land.

One soldier, they claimed, had received his sentence of transportation with a nod of thanks, then left the court singing, '*Too-ra-loo-ra-lay, I'm off to Botany Bay.*'

Lords Harrington and Castlereagh and many others would not tolerate hearing a single word against Lachlan Macquarie, whom they had all known personally; nor would the King who, as the Prince of Wales, had also known General Macquarie fairly well in earlier days.

Of all the people least affected by these accusations was Lachlan Macquarie himself, because he knew nothing about them; but Lord Bathurst was in a turmoil. As Colonial Secretary he had to *do* something to quieten those complaining politicians, but what?

Then it came to him – an *inquiry!* He would send someone out to New South Wales to conduct an *Official Inquiry* into the state of the Colony. That usually kept the bleaters quiet for a time, and would also save him the bother of having to respond to their irritating questions in the House until – 'the *official Inquiry* is completed.'

Although, Bathurst was a wily enough politician himself to know that he had to cover his own back from all sides. So when giving his final instructions to the man that Whitehall had chosen to carry out the Inquiry, Commissioner John Bigge, Lord Bathurst warned him sternly:

'Under no circumstances are you to let Governor Macquarie know the real reason for your arrival in New South Wales. Under no circumstances is he to know that this is an *official* inquiry into his governorship on behalf of the Colonial office.'

'So what *is* the main purpose of my inquiry,' Bigge asked, 'underneath the *official* reason of a routine inquiry into how the settlement is progressing?'

'The main purpose of your inquiry is to find out if New South Wales still fulfils its purpose as a penal colony for felons. Transportation should be a sentence that every felon fears, and therefore it should act as a terrifying deterrent. New South

Wales is an outdoor prison camp, a receptacle for offenders, but is Governor Macquarie running it as such? That is what we need to know.'

'And the emancipists?'

'The emancipists are a *very* thorny issue,' Bathurst replied. 'It's because of his treatment of the emancipists that we are having this inquiry. Macquarie claims to have selected people for top civic posts according to their *merit* and *ability* – surveyors, architects, doctors – stating that many of the free settlers do not possess the knowledge or ability needed for such posts, so I shall look forward to your own unbiased view on that, Mr Bigge.'

'Yes, my lord.'

*

The 'unbiased' face that Commissioner John Bigge had shown so artfully to Lord Bathurst was a false face. He had no intention of supporting any Governor who was too soft on the lower classes of humanity.

And Bathurst knew that. How could he not know it? John Bigge had been chosen for this commission due to his background as a law graduate from Christ Church, Oxford – as was Henry Goulburn – undersecretary to Bathurst. That was his first step inside the door. The second was his colonial experience in the West Indies – and a man reputed to have been ruthlessly tough on colonial slaves was unlikely to be soft on convicts or ex-convicts. Lord Bathurst was sure of that.

At the same time, in the opinion of John Bigge, Lord Bathurst was every bit as deceitful as his political masters, but they were paying him a fat yearly salary to carry out this inquiry – much more than the yearly salary they were paying Governor Macquarie to rule the colony. So, adding all these things together, John Bigge was in no doubt about the report the Colonial Office wanted him to bring back to them from New South Wales.

Not that John Bigge would find it too difficult to do their bidding. Having already read through some of the governor's dispatches and documents about New South Wales, John Bigge concluded that his sympathies lay solely with the free settlers, and not – most certainly not – with Governor Macquarie.

Now 39 years old, John Thomas Bigge came from a Whiggish family in Northumberland – a family that aspired to be as gentrified as the true Tory aristocrats of that northern county, while looking down on the lower order of the inhabitants – and in that respect and with those social pretensions, John Bigge had much in common with the Exclusives in New South Wales.

A bachelor of pernickety tastes and fastidious manners, of average height and light build, his face had a softness in its features that did not support his strong, prominent nose.

It was a face that was known well to the people

in the plantation colony of Trinidad where he had previously served as Chief Justice for five years, and where armies of black slaves toiled for their white masters in producing one-third of the British Empire's sugar, as well as earning enormous profits for the absentee British landlords of huge estates which were run by overseers and their henchmen who were experts in the use of the whip, the dogs, and the cage.

At the time John Bigge had been Chief Justice there, Trinidad had been, and still was, a society of severe punishment and exploitation of over 350,000 slaves, a society in which John Bigge had lived for five years as a practitioner of justice, and served out that justice with such distinction he received a commendation from the governor.

And this was the man considered the most suitable to lead an official inquiry into Lachlan Macquarie's '*paternal*' governorship of a convict colony in New South Wales.

*

In Australia, coincidentally, and blissfully ignorant of what lay ahead, Lachlan Macquarie was busy overseeing the construction of a new town he was building, and which he had already officially named *Wilberforce* – in honour of William Wilberforce who, for years, had been pleading in the British Parliament for the abolition of slavery in all of His Majesty's dominions.

'Do you think Wilberforce will succeed?' George

Jarvis asked.

Lachlan nodded. 'Yes, I think he will, eventually.'

After a pause, George said ruefully, 'I don't think he will, no matter how hard he tries. There is too much of it, all over the world, too much slavery.'

Lachlan was in too much of a good mood to disagree, now that he could see the town taking shape.

'Well, whether he succeeds or not, George, the people of Australia need this new town, and what better or more deserving man to name it in honour of, than a great man like William Wilberforce.'

As they headed back to their military-style white tents near the site of the town, Lachlan added, 'And it's not just Wilberforce who is making the fight against slavery, George, he now has a growing force of similar-minded abolitionists supporting him. Men of influence dedicated to their cause. They will succeed in the end, I am certain of it.'

After a long silence, George said quietly, 'I hope so.'

Chapter Twenty-Nine

The Governor and his party had been away for two weeks, causing Mary Neely to go through her days restless and miserable. Every day without a chance of seeing George Jarvis seemed as long as a year.

Every evening she walked alone through the private gardens at the back of Government House and fed her memories.

Here, on this path, he had spoken to her of the poetry of Khayaam.

And here, he had plucked a red rose and given it to her. All roses had originated in the East, he had told her. All the roses all over the world had descended from the Persian rose.

So many evenings, and so many walks when her love for him had grown stronger and stronger. Maybe it was because he was foreign and different that she always seemed to see him through an enchanted haze. But he was beautiful, so beautiful.

And here, down this path here, just a few nights before he had gone with the governor to Wilberforce, they had strolled side by side in silence for some time, as if talk was unnecessary, as if just being in each other's company again was more than enough.

But for her, it was no longer enough. The physical need burning inside her had become a constant ache.

And then here, at the end of this path, he had

turned to go back ... it was deep twilight, but knowing how darkness falls so suddenly in Australia he put his hand on her arm to guide her, and she stopped and stared up into his eyes, her heart bursting, and all she could say shakily was, 'Oh, George ...'

In the silence he did not move nor question her, as if he didn't need to. She lifted her face up until their lips were just a few inches apart and again she said shakily, 'Oh, George ...'

It was not until he kissed her and his arms closed tightly around her waist that she knew he felt the same love and passion for her that she felt for him, so long unspoken and restrained by both of them.

The brief twilight suddenly vanished into night and it was heaven in the darkness, heaven in this garden of sweet smells and happiness, heaven to feel his lips on her neck and his hands holding her body as if he couldn't bear to let her go.

And he might not have let her go, if a night animal had not rushed past them in the darkness and a bird in a branch some way off had not sent out a piercing squawking screech which seemed to bring George back to his senses and he suddenly moved her away from him, holding her at arm's length saying seriously, 'I think we should go back ... I think that was Mrs Ovens calling you.'

She half laughed in her disappointment. 'George, that was a parrot! And you know it was.'

'Well, it sounded like Mrs Ovens to me,' he said,

and took her hand to lead her out of the heavenly darkness of the garden and back to the lights of the house.

And the following morning he was gone, at the crack of dawn as usual, because Governor Macquarie always liked to start his day early.

She walked in loneliness back through the empty garden to the house, despondency in every line of her figure, as it had been since the day George had left.

In the days that followed her thoughts wandered as she lost herself in wonderful dreams, love being an absorbing passion.

Silent and languid, she carried out her duties with calm efficiency, but seemed so low in energy that Elizabeth looked at her keenly.

'Mary, is there something on your mind ... something that is distracting you?'

Mary looked up, a blushing colour coming in her face, making her look very young and very sweet, and her wonderful golden hair was just beautiful. Oh, how Elizabeth envied that glorious hair.

'Ma'am?'

'Are you not well?'

'I have a slight headache,' Mary confessed.

'Would you like to take a short nap?'

'Oh no, thank you, Ma'am, I would prefer to keep busy.'

For some moments silence reigned, but all the while Elizabeth's eyes remained on Mary's face. She had been a spirited and angry girl when she had first arrived here, angry at the injustice of her transportation, but over time that anger had faded and Mary had changed into a calm and happy girl ... and Elizabeth knew why.

Smiling, Elizabeth reached across the table to pat Mary's hand. 'Never mind, dear, the Governor will be back soon.'

*

'Now look here, m'girl, you've got to stop all this moodiness of yours,' Mrs Ovens chided. 'Not a word can anyone get out of you these days, too wrapped up in yourself, and where's the fun for us in that?'

Mary had entered the kitchen to refill her water glass before going to bed, hoping the kitchen would be empty, allowing her to slip in and out, but Mrs Kelly had come over from her own kitchen and the two cooks were plonked at the table together in preparation for their nightly chat and rum.

'I've been busy,' Mary replied.

'Oh, ay-up, hear that, Mrs Kelly? I don't like your tone, Mary,' Mrs Ovens remonstrated. 'Busy? Too busy to talk to me now, eh? Oh, you're getting airs above your station, girl, all this time upstairs with m'lady has turned your head.'

Mrs Ovens took a quick gulp of her rum – for some reason it was making her very annoyed at life tonight instead of soothing her. Or maybe it was just this damnable heat!

'And remember, m'ducky, if I was to make

complaints to m'lady about you, it wouldn't be those pretty colourful frocks you'd be wearing every day – it'd be straight back to Mrs Kelly's kitchen and you back to wearing convict's yellow, same as all the other girls over there.'

Glass in hand, Mary stared stunned at Mrs Ovens, her face white to her lips.

'And what would your handsome hero think of you when he saw you in that, eh?' Mrs Ovens asked crankily. 'You was already upstairs and wearing one of the dresses m'lady gave you when he first saw you, wasn't you?'

A second later the glass slipped from Mary's hand and fell to the floor. Never again could she bear to wear that repulsive convict's yellow.

'Handsome hero?' Mrs Kelly sat forward. 'What handsome hero? You've told me nothing about this, Mrs Ovens! Who is he?'

But Mrs Ovens wasn't listening to Mrs Kelly, she was staring down at the broken glass on the floor and then up at the tears flowing down Mary's face.

'What's to-do now, Mary, what's to-do?' cried Mrs Ovens in alarm. 'Why're you crying like that – who's upset you?'

'It's him – that George Jarvis,' Mrs Kelly butted in, sudden realising. 'He's the handsome hero! He's the one that's broken Mary's heart and made her tears flow like a river.'

Mary wiped a hand over the tears on her face. 'He knows I'm a convict ...'

'Course he knows,' said Mrs Ovens, 'same as

everyone else knows you're a convict. That's why I warned you not to get too attached to him.'

This only made the tears in Mary's eyes flow even faster. Mrs Ovens jumped to her feet and went over to her. 'Oh, come on now, m'lovey, come on now ... you know I was only teasing about complaining to m'lady and getting you sent back to the kitchen!'

She made Mary sit down on a chair and then lifted her apron and began to gently wipe Mary's eyes and wet face with it. 'There now, m'lovey, there now ...'

'And look at the way that George Jarvis treated poor Rachel,' Mrs Kelly butted in, still in her own world of suspicious thoughts. 'He treated poor Rachel something disgraceful he did.'

Mary pushed Mrs Ovens hand and apron away – her blue eyes staring at Mrs Kelly in shock.

'George and Rachel? In what way did he treat Rachel something disgraceful?'

'By ignoring her completely, as if she wasn't there, always too busy to even notice her. And I tell you, Mary, it was only due to my own long nights of prayers that Rachel finally fell in love with that soldier from the 73rd instead.'

'What soldier is this?' Mrs Oven asked eagerly, sniffing a new romance in the air. 'He's not an officer is he?'

'Don't be daft,' Mrs Kelly tutted. 'No officer would have anything to do with a convict girl. No, he's just a soldier, a regular soldier, looking for a girl he can love and leave ...'

Mary left them to it, gossiping away, but when she reached her small room and sat on her bed, reality hit her hard, and she was no longer a dreaming girl in love, just a servant, a *convict* servant.

*

Two days later a messenger arrived by horse informing Elizabeth that Governor Macquarie would be returning the following morning.

And with that news Government House immediately came alive and busy. Maids fluttering here and there with dusters, gardeners more brisk in their work in the gardens; Mrs Ovens in a flap in the kitchen making meringues and whipping cream and experimenting with a new sauce supposed to taste delicious with wild duck. Everywhere there were happenings; everyone stirred up with more life in them, because the Governor was coming back.

He came back the next morning. February was the hottest month of summer and the heat of the day was already rising. All the windows were open onto the gardens and the sweet scent of summer roses permeated the air inside the house.

As soon as Lachlan entered the hall, Elizabeth greeted him as if he had been away for years. Standing back a few paces Mary dropped a curtsy to Governor Macquarie. He smiled and spoke to her, as he always did, briefly but friendly.

The rest of his party followed him inside and the hall began to fill with people: Major Antill, James Greenway, John Campbell and a number of officers, ... and finally George Jarvis who had been waylaid on the steps by Joseph Bigg and was the last to come into the hall, holding a wooden cage containing a sleepy-eyed parrot with beautiful pink and blue plumage.

'George – you are incorrigible!' Elizabeth laughed, looking at the bird.

'I thought she would make a nice friend for Bappoo,' George replied. 'A friend who might appreciate his calls of *"ello darlin"* more than the gardeners do.'

'But, George, what if she learns to say the same thing back?' Elizabeth asked worriedly. 'Did you not think of that? And if the two of them start squawking the same thing to each other all day long then Mr Byrne will certainly find you and probably kill you.'

Laughing, George's eyes turned to Mary, but she looked past him as if he was a stranger, her blue eyes as clear and as blank as the summer sky.

Chapter Thirty

Some later referred to him as '*the Assassin*', a man who had the long arm of Downing Street pushing at his back.

Others viewed him as a welcome saviour, come to rescue them from the despotic rule of Lachlan Macquarie.

And these 'others' were the Exclusives.

The convict ship carrying the dispatch informing Governor Macquarie of Commissioner John Bigge's journey from England to Australia reached Sydney only five days before the man himself.

The Governor was happy to meet and greet him and, following protocol, thirteen guns fired a salute from Dawes Point, as the guns always did when a government emissary arrived.

Accompanied by his assistant, Thomas Hobbs Scott, who was also his brother-in-law, Commissioner Bigge found himself sitting down to dinner and being entertained warmly by Governor Macquarie and his wife.

Although when Elizabeth withdrew and left the men to themselves, Lachlan felt compelled to ask John Bigge, 'And for what reason, precisely, have you come to Australia?'

John Bigge answered smoothly, 'I have been commissioned to carry out an inquiry into the laws, regulations and usages of the penal settlements of New South Wales and Van Diemen's

Land, on behalf of the British government.'

Lachlan was puzzled. 'And the object of your inquiry is to ascertain ... what?'

'If New South Wales is fulfilling its purpose as a penal colony.'

Astonished, Lachlan half laughed. 'I should think the British government knows very well the answer to that, in view of the fact that they have sent us *seventeen* convict transport ships in the past nine months alone, containing over three thousand convicts, and the number of those transport ships arriving at our shores are increasing by greater numbers every year.'

'Ah, yes ...' John Bigge glanced at his brother-in-law, 'but are the felons being *punished* properly when they arrive here, Governor Macquarie? That is what the British government wants to know.'

And in that moment Lachlan knew who had instigated and caused the need for this inquiry – the Exclusives. And he also saw in that moment that John Bigge was one of their type.

'No doubt you will wish to speak to as many of the inhabitants as freely you can,' Lachlan said finally. 'I will put my carriage driver at your service from tomorrow morning.'

*

'We will see which of the inhabitants, and which of the homesteads he chooses to visit first,' Lachlan said later to Elizabeth in the bedroom, 'exclusive or emancipist?'

'I disliked him on sight,' Elizabeth confessed. 'And the more I saw of him, the more I disliked him ... something about him. The delicate way he handled his knife and fork, the finicky way he removed all the fat from the lamb cutlets ... and his soft hand when he held mine, as soft as a baby's hand, and his softly smooth voice ... yet his eyes were as cold and as hard as rocks. Did you notice? His cold eyes?'

'No, I didn't notice,' Lachlan replied offhandedly, not interested in the physical appearance of the man. It was the *intentions* of the commissioner that he was interested in, and what *information* he was hoping to gain, and – most importantly – to whom he would go to first when seeking that information.

That is why he had offered the services of his own carriage driver to the commissioner.

*

The following morning, Joseph Bigg, sitting on the driver's bench of the governor's carriage, chucked the reins and set off with the commissioner and his assistant seated comfortably inside.

'See you tonight, m'lady,' Joseph said as he tipped his hat to Elizabeth.

But Joseph Bigg did not return with the carriage that night, or the following night.

When he finally returned with the carriage three nights later, Lachlan asked him, 'Who was the first person the commissioner went to visit?'

'John McArthur.'

'And where is the commissioner now?'

'Over at Reverend Marsden's place, staying there a few days, so 'e sent me and the carriage back.'

When Joseph had gone, Lachlan slowly turned to look at George Jarvis. 'The snakes are coiling and hissing, George.'

George's eyes were dark with anger and disgust. 'And soon they will be rattling in readiness to attack you.'

'No doubt'

'So what are you going to do?'

Lachlan shrugged. 'What I always do, George, ignore them and get on with the bloody job.'

Chapter Thirty-One

Commissioner John Bigge had great sympathy for the free settlers of the colony, being denied by Governor Macquarie all the rights that their free status entitled them to. No use of the whip? No flogging without the consent and order of a magistrate? It was not only ridiculous, it was madness – he thought back to his years in Trinidad – how on earth could order have been maintained on that island of so many slaves without the use of the whip?

Reverend Marsden, he believed to be a good and devout man, and his wish to convert the Maoris in New Zealand to Christianity was admirable, although it was highly regrettable that Governor Macquarie had so far denied him the finances, soldiers and sailing vessel to carry out that mission.

Those other free settlers he had met were somewhat dull, although quite bearable, but the man who impressed him the most was John McArthur.

John McArthur's view of the colony was much more in line with that of the Colonial Office and the British government. Now that the Blue Mountains had been opened up with roads into a vast interior, John McArthur could see the possibility of thousands of sheep grazing on those rich green pastures.

Endless land, vast sheep farms, and later *millions* of sheep for as far as the eyes could see – allowing the wool barons to supply Britain with all the cheap wool it needed for its own use and exports.

But for that vision to become a possibility, the government would need to release that land to the sheep farmers, as well as supplying vast numbers of convict labour as a workforce.

Commissioner Bigge agreed with McArthur's vision. The sheep farms worked by convict labour could be run just like the British sugar plantations worked by slaves in Trinidad.

Yet Governor Macquarie, the ruler of the colony, seemed more interested in improving the lives and conditions for emancipists and convict felons.

'And while he continues to do so,' John McArthur said ruefully to the commissioner, 'I fear my flocks must remain static, unless an unexpected change should be made in the system of *managing* prisoners.'

And that change would come, Commissioner Bigge was determined it would.

He sat down and wrote yet another letter to Lord Bathurst, pointing out that so far the colony of New South Wales exported nothing more than bills to the Treasury to pay for the upkeep of the colony, the military and the convicts – *'an estimated £150,000 a year, I am told.'*

When Commissioner Bigge later mentioned this exorbitant amount of money to Governor

Macquarie, insisting it to be 'a very *high* cost to Britain!'

Lachlan replied, 'If Britain wishes the cost of running this country to be kept as low as possible, then surely the best way to achieve that is for Britain to stop sending shiploads of British convicts out to this country.'

'But, your Excellency ...' Commissioner Bigge's mouth was turned down, 'this *is* a *penal* colony.'

'Yes, and when I first arrived in this country nine years ago, there were no more than seven thousand convicts here. Yet now there are over *thirty thousand* convicts here and more arriving by the shipload every few months. So how am I supposed to house and feed all these extra convicts and still keep the bills the same?'

'But surely the convict labour can be put to better use?'

'Better use ... what better use?' Lachlan was beginning to lose control of his temper with this pursed-lip little man. 'When I arrived in Sydney it was little more than a hovel of shacks with no amenities, no common buildings and no roads of any description, just dirt tracks. The only decent habitations were Government House and those houses built by the free settlers using convict labour.

'Lachlan ...' Elizabeth could see her husband was losing his temper and put out her hand to warn him that he was.

'But now,' Lachlan continued, 'thanks to the

hard work of that convict labour, Sydney is now a city suitable enough to welcome even a gentleman like yourself, Commissioner Bigge, with every amenity necessary, such as a fully functioning hospital, and two schools to educate the young.'

'And a separate school to educate the black *Aboriginal* children as well!' the commissioner retorted with eyebrows high. 'I did not realise that educating the black savages in this land was a part of your remit from the King, Governor Macquarie!'

For one long silent moment Lachlan Macquarie stared at John Bigge, then he quietly pushed back his chair and stood up, and without haste or any change of expression on his face, walked out of the room.

It was an end to the conversation and a dismissal, and John Bigge knew it was. His red cheeks showed his embarrassment.

Elizabeth also rose to her feet, her expression and voice ice-cold. 'Dinner appears to be over, Commissioner Bigge. Thank you so much for coming. Goodnight.'

And she too swept out of the room, leaving Commissioner Bigge alone with his half-eaten dinner.

A half-eaten dinner which he left behind him, preferring instead to spend the rest of the evening writing a letter of complaint about Governor Macquarie to the Colonial Office.

Chapter Thirty-Two

For months and months Mary had not gone anywhere near the gardens in the evening time.

For months and months she had avoided George Jarvis, refusing to meet his eyes whenever she had to enter the governor's office or apartments. And all of those times when he had tried to speak to her in corridors or on landings she had not listened to him, carrying on with whatever she was doing as if she was deaf.

And then he had stopped trying, and seemed to spend most of his time avoiding her, which was not too difficult for George, due to his having accompanied Governor Macquarie on yet another of his three-month trips to Van Diemen's Land to make sure his building programmes there were progressing satisfactorily, especially his new school and hospital.

Lately, Mary had taken to spending some of her evenings in the company of Mrs Ovens and Mrs Kelly, sipping more and more of their rum until she was almost as drunk as they were.

But rum was like water to those two, and didn't seem to have the same effect on them as it did on her.

And tonight she was drunk, good and drunk, or at least she thought she was.

Mrs Ovens laughed. 'You've only had a few more sips than normal, so what makes you say you're drunk! And listen, m'girl, it's not good for females to drink too much rum, it's unladylike.'

'So why do you two drink rum – *all* the time – *every* night!'

'It's different for us,' Mrs Kelly informed her. 'We're older and past caring.'

'And widowed,' Mrs Ovens added. 'Both of us! And stuck out here in a convict colony. So why wouldn't we drink?'

'By God, you're right!' Mrs Kelly exclaimed sorrowfully. 'Widowed and stuck out here in a convict colony – here, give me some more of that rum!'

Mrs Ovens poured out two good measures from the jug of rum and the two cooks touched their glasses together.

'I want a drink too!' Mary demanded.

Mrs Ovens lowered the glass from her mouth, smacked her lips appreciatively, and then looked at Mary with narrowed eyes.

'Why do you have the need to drink these nights, Mary? You would never touch a drop before.'

'I want another drink!' Mary insisted.

'Then will you tell us?' Mrs Kelly asked her. 'If we give you another drink will you tell us why you need it?'

Mary nodded.

Mrs Ovens poured her the usual tiny measure then watched as Mary knocked it back in one gulp, making her entire body shudder afterwards.

'So?' Mrs Ovens asked.

'I drink because I'm a convict.'

The two cooks looked at each other, and then burst out laughing.

'Go away with you!' said Mrs Kelly. 'That's not the reason. You was a convict before and you didn't need to drink, so what's the *real* reason?'

'I drink because I'm miserable.'

'And why are you miserable?' asked Mrs Ovens.

'I'm miserable because I drink.'

Mrs Kelly looked at Mrs Ovens. 'Maybe she is drunk? It's the only explanation for talking such nonsense.'

Mary suddenly stood up and walked like a sleepwalker out of the kitchen. Those two would never be able to understand her ravaging heartache.

*

A few weeks later Governor Macquarie returned from Van Diemen's Land, but it was not until days after the return that Mary saw George again – from her window.

He was walking slowly in the garden, and her heart leaped. Was he waiting for her there, hoping to meet her there?

But leaning forward, she saw he was not, because he was holding the hand of Lachlan Junior hopping beside him, and then Mrs Macquarie came into view, a short way behind them.

A few paces on, Mrs Macquarie sat down on a garden bench and George turned back and sat down beside her, young Lachlan scrambling onto his lap, and there they sat, Mrs Macquarie and George, talking very seriously together while young Lachlan began to relax into a doze.

She turned her head slowly and looked towards the pack of cards on the small dresser by her bed ... realising how pointless it all was – standing here watching him from the window – because no matter how many times she had shuffled the pack ... hoping, wishing ... it was never to be seen in the cards ... her and George, free and convict, being together, loving each other ... it was never to be seen in the cards.

Still she turned her eyes back to the garden and saw they were still sitting on the bench, still talking to each other, quietly and seriously. At times Mrs Macquarie looked as if she was getting very anxious about something, but as they talked on she began to relax, and Mary couldn't help noticing again the confidence that Mrs Macquarie always seemed to take from George's calm counsel and advice.

Mary Rouse came on the scene, a very pretty girl, one of the new maids in the nursery, but *she* was not a convict, no, she was the daughter of Richard Rouse, an emancipist who was now a leading resident out at Parramatta.

Mary Rouse moved to lift young Lachlan from George's lap and arms, but George raised his hand to stop her, obviously saying that he would carry the sleeping child back into the house.

Mrs Macquarie made a gesture with her hand and nodded her head as if saying she wished to remain where she was for a while, and Mary watched as George and the new maid strolled back towards the house, talking and smiling together in a very friendly way.

The feeling inside her, caused by the sight of the two of them so friendly together, was unbearable. And how *dare* she – that Mary Rouse? Lachlan Junior was *her* charge, so who was Mary Rouse to go walking into the garden to take him? Whether he was asleep or not, it was not her place to do so – and how did she *know* he was asleep, if she had not been watching from a window also.

Impulsively she turned and fled out of her room and along the landing and down the stairs until she was in the hallway, running to meet the two of them as they came into the hall and then reaching to take young Lachlan from George's arms.

'Mary, you will wake him,' George said in surprised alarm.

'He's *my* charge,' Mary insisted, taking the child into her own arms, and then turning a haughty look at Mary Rouse. 'And weren't *you* supposed to be doing his laundry?'

Mary Rouse turned a deep red and then bowed her head and rushed down the hall as if looking for somewhere to hide and die.

George was looking at Mary in puzzlement. Never before had he heard her speak to another maid like that, and it was not in her nature to be cold and cruel.

'There was no need to speak to her like that,' he said quietly.

'Why not – because she's a *currency* girl and not a convict?'

Her breath was heaving and her blue eyes were flashing with an anger he had not seen since the old days when she dreamed of murdering her mistress in England.

'What's wrong, Mary? Why have you changed these past months and gone away somewhere inside your head where no one can reach you?'

'I have *not* changed, I am *still* a convict.'

The anger in her voice caused young Lachlan to wake up and start to bawl at his rude awakening, wriggling down from Mary's arms and running down the hall looking for his mama, with Mary running after him.

George watched her go, still puzzled. Her face had been so pale, and whenever he had seen her of late there had been dark shadows under her eyes as if she was not sleeping, and those dark shadows were still there. What had happened to her? What had changed her?

And what of his own jumbled thoughts? He needed and deserved some sort of clarification from her if only to help him understand what had gone wrong between them. His mind and emotions had been taxed so much during these past months that he realised it was now imperative to make her speak to him in order to give him some explanation that could lead to a solution or a final conclusion of their relationship.

Because it was not concluded, not yet – he had seen that today, on her face, and in the way she had spoken so severely to Mary Rouse with burning fury in her eyes.

And all young Mary Rouse had been doing was responding to his questions and telling him that Mary now often spent some of her evenings in one of the kitchens with the two cooks.

*

The glasses were on the table, the rum already poured, and Mrs Ovens was urging Mrs Kelly to tell Mary another tale about her handsome lover back in Ireland.

'Oh!' cried Mrs Kelly. 'Will I ever forget him?'

'No, you won't ever forget him, if you *never* stop talking about him,' Mary said tiredly.

But Mrs Kelly's mind was already back in the small cottage hidden within lush green woodlands where only the love songs of the lark and the nightingale disturbed the peace, until *he* came a-calling that sweet summer's day ...

Mary had not asked for even a sip of the rum tonight but she did not want to be alone with her thoughts, so annoyed was she with herself at the awful way she had spoken to Mary Rouse today and the jealous face she had shown to George.

She dropped her face on her folded arms on the table and closed her tired eyes as she began to listen to one more of Mrs Kelly's boring stories about her Irish lover, yet Mrs Ovens, the old romantic, couldn't seem to hear enough of them.

At least Mrs Ovens had stopped questioning her about George Jarvis, wanting to know why she never saw them together anymore; and Mrs Kelly had stopped telling her she was right to have nothing to do with him; and she had let them talk and had answered none of their questions, because she didn't expect either of those two old women to understand her love for George, or her need for him ... but she did need him ... every time she saw him she felt her need for him ... and she did miss him now, so much ...

'And there was I,' said Mrs Kelly, 'sitting on the top bar of the gate of the field, and he puts his hands under both my armpits, close to my breasts, and begins to slowly lift me down to the ground...' she paused to shiver deliciously.

George Jarvis entered the kitchen and walked straight over to Mary and saw she had fallen asleep. He gently shook her shoulder to wake her and when she lifted her head to look at him with sleepy eyes he said, 'Mary, I need to talk with you.'

'What's this, what's this...?' cried Mrs Ovens, and her shocked voice brought Mrs Kelly back to reality with blinking eyes, and then seeing George standing there, she jumped to her feet to quickly cover the illicit jug of rum with the lower half of her apron.

'What – *you* shouldn't be in here, George Jarvis,'

Mrs Kelly declared defensively, 'This is *my* kitchen and you've no right to come in here without a warrant!'

George was looking down into Mary's upturned face. 'Will you come with me for a walk in the garden?'

Mary nodded and rose from her chair and started walking towards the back door.

'Now see here, George Jarvis,' Mrs Kelly warned. 'You know Governor Macquarie don't like no finagling between the sexes in his household.'

George paused, and looked towards the jug that Mrs Kelly was hiding under her apron. 'Is that a jug of rum? *Rum?* In one of the kitchens of the governor's household?'

'Go on with you!' Mrs Oven chuckled. 'You know it's only water, George.'

'You two –' he said, pointing at both of them. 'If you try to question Mary when she returns, then I may have to tell the governor that I'm certain it *is* rum.'

'Now I knows you'd do no such thing, George!' Mrs Ovens laughed, and she was still laughing to herself when George walked out.

She wriggled in her chair to lean closer to Mrs Kelly and said excitedly, 'There's going to be either some trouble or some lovemaking between those two tonight, unless I'm very much mistook!'

Chapter Thirty-Three

No sunset as always, just a sudden change from daylight to night and the bright rising of the moon.

Mary was almost at the garden. She turned round and saw George walking towards her, not rushing to catch up with her, just walking towards her in his usual calm and steady way.

'What is it?' she asked quietly. 'Why do you want to talk to me?'

He looked at her with an anxious look. Always in the past she had been full of vitality and lightness, but this evening she drooped listlessly. Only her beautiful pale hair, which hung loose down her back, retained its shine as if in defiance of her mood.

'I need to know what has changed. Why you seem to have so much silent anger inside you. Why you lower your eyes or turn your back whenever you see me. Why? Have you been told something bad about me?'

'Oh George,' she smiled faintly. 'Everyone knows there is nothing bad about you.'

'Even Mrs Kelly?'

'Even Mrs Kelly ... she just pretends to dislike you because you are handsome and polite and make her think of her unfaithful Irish lover.'

'Then what has caused it, this change in you? What have I done wrong?'

'Oh, George, you've done nothing wrong, and

I've done nothing wrong ... all I did was borrow a small mirror from my mistress's bedroom, just for a few minutes ... ' Tears were coming into her eyes, she turned away and began to walk slowly along the garden path.

'You and I, George, it's all so pointless. All the meetings on the landings and the walks in this garden ... all so pointless.'

'Why is it pointless?'

'Because you are such an important man here in Government House, and so important to Governor Macquarie that he rarely goes anywhere without you. Even the officers treat you with so much respect. But me ... I'm just a convict, a low felon convict ... I could never be good enough for you.'

'Never be good enough for me? Mary, you know nothing about me.'

'I know you have never been a convict on a transport ship with rusty irons on your ankles.'

'No, but I have been a *slave,* bought and sold many times, with a tight rope around my waist.'

Mary turned to him, her eyes wide with shock. 'But Mrs Macquarie told me that when you were young ... you were the son of a prince.'

'Yes, the son of a prince, but also the child of a captured slave-girl sold to that prince, before she was sold again.'

Mary was so stunned she had to lean back against a tree. 'And Governor Macquarie ...'

'Rescued me, when I was about seven or eight years old. He was a young soldier then, but he has been my true father ever since.'

'But ... your name is not Macquarie ... it's Jarvis.'

George closed his eyes and shook his head. 'This is not the time ... '

And again, as he so often had done in the past, when he needed a moment alone to think to himself, he slowly walked away from her, further down the path, and then stopped and stood looking up at the sky and the moon as if trying to make a decision.

She watched him, her chest choking with emotion and annoyance at her own stupidity, her own self-pity about being a convict, which had made him tell her things about himself which he had probably never told to any other person in the world outside the Macquarie family ... yet now he had told her ... why? And was he already regretting it, and that's why he had walked away from her?

Trembling with fear, she took a step away from the tree and whispered, 'George?'

He turned his head and looked at her, and then began slowly to walk back towards her, saying softly, 'The only thing we really know is the truth ... I love you, Mary ... and in the past months I have felt as far away from you as the earth is from heaven.'

She moved to him in the warm moonlight and put her arms around his neck and hugged him so lovingly all further speech was unnecessary.

*

Mrs Kelly and Mrs Ovens were still in the kitchen, slumped opposite each other at the table, nursing the last few drops of the jug of rum.

'Well, if we're going to find out what he wanted to talk to her about, she'll have to hurry up and get back quick,' Mrs Kelly said tiredly. 'It's long past my bedtime so it is.'

Mrs Ovens nodded. 'Maybe she went back in through the side door so as not to tell us. Or maybe it was all nothing worth talking about. Maybe I was mistook.'

Mrs Kelly blinked blearily at her empty glass, and then stretched her hand out vaguely towards the empty rum jug.

'The only one who was mistook was him – warning us not to ask Mary any questions about it. What kind of women does he think we are – dead?'

*

Two candles were still burning in George's bedroom, the warm night air coming through the open window causing their lights to flicker over her body, the slender beautiful body she had given to him so willingly, her words like unintelligible whispered prayers as he loved her, lost himself in her splendour, and then loved her again.

Now she lay very still, her eyes closed, her breathing calm, and when he eventually laid his hand softly on her shoulder, she opened her blue eyes and came awake as if from a dream.

Her voice just a faint whisper, she asked, 'How

long have we been here?'

He didn't know. 'An hour, maybe two.'

Her eyes closed again as she whispered, 'An hour, maybe two ... in heaven.'

Chapter Thirty-Four

The letters of complaints from Exclusives in New South Wales had been endlessly pouring into the Colonial Office in London, and one letter, in particular, had infuriated Lord Bathurst.

The writer of the letter had withheld his or her signature and address, remaining anonymous, but the gross charge against Governor Macquarie in that letter, had also been hinted at in other letters from New South Wales.

Too angry to detail the contents of the letter himself, Lord Bathurst simply enclosed the anonymous letter in a dispatch to Governor Macquarie, demanding an explanation and an answer to this grotesque charge against him.

And now that dispatch from the Colonial Office had arrived at its destination and was being read by the King's Viceroy in Sydney.

As Lachlan read through the anonymous letter that Bathurst had enclosed, his eyes opened wider and wider, unable to believe it – every word it contained was the exact opposite to the truth.

And the fact that Lord Bathurst should not only give credence to such a malicious letter, but also demand that the Governor should be held in question to it, filled Lachlan with a cold fury he could barely contain. He thought long and hard before replying to Lord Bathurst.

I thank your Lordship for sending me the Anonymous letter, in order to give me the opportunity of refuting the false and malicious accusation therein contained.

First – the state of Prostitution in which it is stated that the Female Convicts, during their voyage out to this Country, are permitted to live with the Officers and Seamen of the ships.

I need only reply to your Lordship with the Question – How is it possible that I, dwelling in New South Wales, can prevent or be answerable for the Prostitution of Female Convicts antecedent to their arrival within my Government?

When the female convicts arrive, they are mustered by my Secretary John Campbell on board Ship, and the usual questions are put to them in regard to their good or bad treatment during the voyage; and if they appear healthy, and do not complain of ill usage, they are either assigned to such Married persons as require them for domestic servants, or are sent to work at the Government Female Factory at Parramatta.

I have never for an instant, directly or by connivance, sanctioned or allowed Prostitution by female convicts after their arrival in this Country.

But thoroughly sick now of the bitter and endless

class war, and the continuous malicious attacks upon his character, which Bathurst had sought to question, he enclosed with the letter his official Resignation of the Office of Governor-General of New South Wales.

And this time, he made it very clear, he would accept no refusal.

*

Elizabeth was also furious when she read the anonymous letter, drawing in her breath and then referring to *'that pack of villains'* as the worst on God's earth.

But later, when her fury had subsided, she felt very sad about Lachlan's resignation, considering his future absence to be a great loss to this country of Australia, the land he had loved, the land he had named.

And she, too, loved this country, this sunny country, the sunniest country in the world with all of its boundless opportunities.

In the future, she had no doubt, that men like John McArthur and Reverend Marsden would rule this country and reap great wealth from it – but it would be the *emancipist* population who would turn out the best.

Of that she was certain.

Even now she could see it. See how it was the *emancipist* parents who kept warning their children *'not to break the law.'* A law they had fallen foul of, and for them it had been a foul law too.

Later that evening, lost in her thoughts, sitting in a chair by the window overlooking the front garden and watching her tame wallabies, she suddenly turned her head and said to Lachlan:

'That pack of villains ... have you noticed how when speaking, and even in their letters, they always still refer to this place as a *colony,* and never a *country,* as we do.'

'That's because they are short-sighted and can't see beyond their own stations,' Lachlan replied. 'They think human beings can be herded and made as obedient as sheep, which is impossible. And their interests travel no further than their own bank accounts.'

'In the bank that *you* had built and opened for them. The Bank of New South Wales.'

Lachlan shrugged. 'Every city needs a bank, and so does every business.'

He looked at her. 'But you know, despite my resignation, my own business here must continue. I *must* keep moving forward to complete the projects I've started. So much work still needs to be done here. And until my successor arrives, I intend to spend each day doing what I have always done – get on with the bloody job.'

*

Lachlan kept the news of his resignation secret for many months, knowing it could undermine his authority if it was known that he would soon be vacating his high office.

Only Elizabeth knew.

But eventually Lachlan realised that he would have to confide the fact to George Jarvis, because their lives were so inextricably linked.

George was stunned when Lachlan told him, realising its implications for him personally.

'And you wish me to leave and go back to Britain with you?'

'The choice is yours, George, what I wish is irrelevant.'

Yet George could see in Lachlan's eyes that his choice was far from irrelevant to him. They had been together for so long now, since young man and small boy, always together, and in so many foreign countries. Together.

Silenced by a maelstrom of emotions, George thought back to that promise he had made to Lachlan, so long ago, from a passage he had read in their English Bible ...

> *Wherever thou go, I shall go*
> *Thy people, shall be my people*
> *And thy God, my God ...*

But now George had made promises to someone else, someone he loved even more than he loved Lachlan, his father in all but blood, the man who had raised him.

George also knew that Lachlan's resignation was due solely to the constant attacks against him by the Exclusives – *they* were responsible, *they* had forced him out – and theirs would be the victory.

So how could George leave his father's side now? In his defeat? In his fall from grace, even with the Colonial Office who believed all the lies?

No, no, they had travelled and stood together through many wars, in Cochin, in Egypt, and even in China where Lachlan had suffered the worst defeat of all – not only against the British-hating Chinese Mandarins, but also in the loss of Jane.

No, no, too much had been given to him by both Lachlan and Jane, as well as Elizabeth. He could not, and would not leave them now.

But he could not leave Mary either. She was the star of his life, the sun in his sky, the sweet flower that made every day wonderful. No, he could not leave Mary either.

Yet how could he walk in two different directions at the same time?

*

When, in confidence, George told Mary about Governor Macquarie's resignation, which would lead to his departure from Australia, as well as his own, Mary's heart nearly burst with the pain of it.

'No! No! I'll not stay here without you, George, not in this house or the gardens where I'd keep seeing your ghost all the time.'

Tears began to spill down her face.

'For you, George, just to be near you, just to know you are close by, I would submit myself to any hardship, any punishment, even going back to scrubbing kitchen floors and wearing convict yellow, but this –' she put her hands to her eyes and pressed them as if trying to push the tears back.

He drew her hands down and held them tightly in his own saying, 'You know I love you?'

She nodded, answering through her tears, 'And I know I love you.'

'Then trust me ... I have no intention of leaving you.'

Chapter Thirty-Five

Lachlan turned away and tried to think rationally. As always, he only wanted the best for George Jarvis.

'*She* is the best for me,' George insisted. 'For so long I have been sure of it, but now I am positive, convinced, definite, certain. How many more words must I use to assure you?'

'But she is *a convict,* George.'

The argument in the room brought Elizabeth to the door. She had heard it all, and had never before seen George Jarvis lose his calmness and appear so irate.

Elizabeth looked at her husband. 'May I join in this argument?'

'No,' Lachlan replied tersely. And it's not an argument, it's a discussion.'

'Mary may be a convict,' Elizabeth went on, undeterred, 'but her only crime was to borrow a mirror without asking her mistress's permission. And apart from that small misdemeanour, for which she has already been more than severely punished, she is still a nice and decent girl in every way. You have said so yourself.'

Lachlan looked at his wife. 'So? What are you saying?'

'He is saying that Mary is not good enough for me,' George snapped.

'No, George, he is not saying that,' Elizabeth

responded steadily. 'He is saying that Mary is a convicted felon, and there are laws concerning free persons and convicts entering into marriage. Laws that must be upheld, especially by the man who heads the government here.'

'Exactly,' Lachlan said, 'that's what I've been *trying* to tell him.'

'No, you didn't say it like that,' George argued. 'You just kept saying she is a convict.'

'Because you would not allow me to say anything further before interrupting. And George, whether we like it or not, she *is* a convict, and there lies the problem.'

'Of course,' Elizabeth interjected coolly, 'there is a very simple solution to the problem.'

Lachlan looked at his wife even more uncertainly. 'Which is?'

'To grant Mary a free pardon. You *are* still the Governor here, Lachlan. You hold the law in your hands. And you *have* granted pardons to other convicts for lesser reasons than Mary's monumental achievement of finally making George, in his personal life, content and happy. You could free Mary with a stroke of your pen ... if you truly wanted to.'

Lachlan and George stared at Elizabeth, and then at each other.

'Well ...' Lachlan said slowly and thoughtfully, 'Mary did save my son from breaking his neck in what could have been a fatal fall down the stairs, twisting her ankle badly and risking her own life in doing so ... I suppose that *could* be considered an act of dedicated bravery way beyond her call of duty. Would you say so, Elizabeth?'

'Oh, I would definitely say so. If she had not saved our son, well ... dare we even think about it?'

'And you, George, would you say so?'

George Jarvis was smiling. 'Yes, my father, I would.'

*

One month later, George Jarvis and Mary Neely were married before Reverend Cowper in St Philip's Church in Sydney.

Later that night, when the wedding party was over and the household at Government House had retired to bed, only Mrs Kelly and Mrs Ovens remained up in one of the kitchens.

'Did you see what she did in the church?' Mrs Ovens asked. 'Right there in front of Reverend Cowper? I think it was George who made her do it, and in the church too.'

'I wasn't in the church to see anything, remember? I was over in your kitchen helping to get the food ready. What did she do?'

'Well, it was a good thing there was only Governor and Mrs Macquarie and myself and Joseph Bigg there, if there had been more people looking on it would have been very discomforting to say the least. Things like that don't usually happen at weddings.'

'What things?' Mrs Kelly was getting impatient.

'What did she do?

'Well, after they had made their promises, she then opens her little silk purse that was hanging from her wrist, and from it she takes a pack of cards, and then right there, in front of the alter, she silently tears each card up, one by one, and each card she tore she handed over to George, and then when we came out of the church, George threw the torn pieces up in the air, and Mrs Macquarie laughed and thought it was very funny.'

Mrs Kelly might have thought it funny too, but she was feeling too sad in herself to laugh or find joy or amusement in anything now, because a week previously the news of the Governor's resignation and return to Britain had also been announced and made official.

'When he goes, will you be going too?' she asked Mrs Ovens moodily. 'Back to Britain?'

'Back to dear old London?' Mrs Kelly looked nostalgic for a moment, and then sipped some more of her rum.

'Well now, I've been thinking about it, I have, and what I keeps thinking is this ... if I go back with Governor Macquarie, I'll probably have to live in Scotland, which is a cold place they say.'

'Oh, aye, very cold they say,' Mrs Kelly agreed.

'Mind you, he's got his own big house and estate in Scotland has Governor Macquarie. Jarvisfield it's called, the estate. And so once he goes back there, he'll be the laird of Jarvisfield again.'

'God in Heaven,' Mrs Kelly sighed sadly. 'I wish

he'd just stay and carry on as the laird of Sydney.'

'Me too, m'ducks, me too.'

'So will you just go back to London?'

'And then again, I keeps thinking...' Mrs Ovens continued, 'if I goes back to Lord Harrington's in London, I can see them all now ... a starched housekeeper and her assistant and then her assistant, and the stiff butlers with their white gloves and high noses ... and then when I goes outside its to the crowded and wet London streets with their puddles of rain underfoot and the stenches and urchins and noise which never really bothered me before ...'

She took another sip of rum, a bigger one this time, while Mrs Kelly hung on to her every word without drinking a drop herself.

'And, of course, being older and away for so long, I'd not be given the position of head cook. I'd be one of the assistant cooks under orders. And then at night, in the kitchen ... there'd be the head butler, sitting silently reading *The Times* no doubt, while the parlour maids and chamber maids sat doing their sewing and the like, and it would all be very nice and respectable ... and every night I'd be sitting there by the fire thinking to myself – what the blazes am I doing here sitting staring into a smoky fire when I could be over in the fresh air of sunny Australia having a good gossip and a laugh and a nice glass of rum with my dear friend Mrs Kelly?'

There was a momentary silence before Mrs

Kelly, her voice and face suddenly transformed and glorified with joy, cried out, 'You'll not be leaving then? You'll be staying here with us?'

Mrs Ovens laughed. 'I am, m'ducks, I'm staying right here where I am, and so is Joseph Bigg – he don't want to leave Australia and go back to London neither.'

Chapter Thirty-Six

The Colonial Office had finally allowed Lachlan Macquarie to leave the country he had named Australia after having ruled it as Governor-General for twelve years. In December 1821, Sir Thomas Brisbane arrived to replace him.

Once again Lachlan was aboard a ship looking back – and before him lay all the testimony of his work. The colony of New South Wales, upon his arrival, had been no more than a small shabby settlement around Sydney Cove, the population less than ten thousand, including the regiments. Now it was almost forty thousand.

The land under tillage had increased from 7000 acres to 33,000 acres; and the penetrated area of the country expanded from 2000 square miles to more than 100,000 square miles, all connected by nearly three hundred miles of serviceable roads up and beyond the Blue Mountains.

He had built the townships of Liverpool, Richmond, Bathurst, Campbelltown, Wilberforce and Newcastle, amongst others. He had laid the foundation stone of St Mary's Cathedral, the first Catholic Church in Sydney, and also two Protestant ones. He had established the first Bank of New South Wales, and opened the first public library.

A home had been erected for the blind. He had opened an orphanage for girls, another for boys. The first school for Aboriginal children had been his pet project at Parramatta – although there had been a small degree of embarrassment when a number of the Aboriginal children had passed their exams with greater skill and higher marks than some of the Europeans.

On Macquarie Street he had built a second large and commodious home for young female convicts who had earned their ticket of leave.

True, the Exclusives had been outraged at the handsome house which offered such comfort, but the house was more than just an elegant building and respectable residence – it was a home and safe haven for those girls who had served their time, and it saved them from the necessity of turning to prostitution in order to earn the money to provide a roof over their heads, or earn their boat fare back to Britain.

And for every change he had made, every law he had legislated, every necessary building he had built – the same had been done for the people of Van Diemen's Land also.

And then there were the Aboriginal people of this land.

Four days previously, on the 11th February, he had performed his last public service in New South Wales, when he finally succeeded in settling King Bungaree and his people in the village he named 'George's Head'. It was a pretty place, with a romantic road leading from the beach to the village. And King Bungaree, against all expectations, had been delighted with the farm that Governor Macquarie's team of workers had put in order for the exclusive use of the Aboriginals.

A celebration dinner followed, attended by three hundred and forty Aboriginals, during which King Bungaree had shed tears appreciatively at Governor Macquarie's assurance that he and his people had been strongly recommended to the kind protection of the new viceroy, Sir Thomas Brisbane

And today Bungaree displayed his gratitude in the greatest way he knew how, by leading his people down to Sydney harbour to say farewell to '*Massa Mawarrie*' fully dressed as a chief – in the white breeches and red coat of a general's uniform that Lachlan had given to him.

But now, all but one last farewell was over.

*

The harbour was crowded, not only with the people of Sydney, but numerous others who had travelled far and wide from all parts of the interior just to say their farewells to Lachlan Macquarie, the man they later declared to be: '*The greatest Governor New South Wales has ever known.*'

Every rock on Bennelong Point, and every rock on the western side of the harbour was covered with men, women and children, watching him leave. The entire population, except the Exclusives, were deeply sad to see the end of the Macquarie Era.

Walking past the scarlet lines of soldiers at the harbour, Lachlan finally paused and turned to the crowds to give them his last speech, and final farewell, his voice strong, *'My fellow citizens of Australia –'*

The crowds roared their cheers and it was some minutes before he could continue, cutting his speech short and giving them one last promise:

'I shall not fail, on my return to England, to recommend in the strongest manner to my Sovereign and to His Majesty's Government, to give their attention to this valuable rising country, and to extend to it their paternal support and fostering protection.'

The cheers roared again, and Lachlan and his entourage chose that moment to wave farewell and climb aboard the embarkation barge that would take them out to the ship.

*

'The shores were lined with innumerable spectators,' reported the *Gazette*, *'but on each face was an indication of an emotion too big, too sincere, for utterance.'*

And now, on the deck of the *Surry*, Elizabeth stood next to her husband, clutching the hand of eight-year-old Lachlan who was dressed as a Highlander for the first time, in a suit of tartan.

And by the side of Lachlan senior, as always, stood George Jarvis, with his wife Mary, who was six months pregnant.

As the *Surrey* prepared to set her sails to the wind, all nineteen guns on the Dawes Point Battery thundered out salutes of honour. While in the harbour vast numbers of boats were either sailing or rowing furiously out to the *Surry* to say one more last farewell, surrounding the ship and shouting '*Lachlan Macquarie!*" repeatedly, until Elizabeth dissolved in tears and the ship's commander, Captain Baine, became apprehensive.

'General Macquarie, we must get out to sea before the wind changes,' Captain Baine said anxiously. 'I fear the people will not leave while they still have sight of you. So I think it advisable that you retire to your cabin and remain there until we are out at sea.'

Lachlan lifted his hand to the people in a brief salute, and then turned away and went below deck.

'*Australia,*' reported the Gazette, '*saw her benefactor for the last time, and felt it too!*'

*

For six months after the ship's departure, Happy Howe and his son Robert of the *Gazette,* constantly rushed down to the harbour whenever a new ship came in, to see if any reports or letters had been sent back from the various ports on the route to England from Governor Macquarie.

Only one report came back, in a letter sent by Mrs Macquarie to Mrs Ovens, a report which made Mrs Ovens and Mrs Kelly celebrate with joy, before Joseph Bigg passed the news on to the *Gazette* –

278

when the *Surry* had docked three months earlier at St Salvadore in Brazil, Mary Jarvis had given birth to a daughter, and the *'beautiful baby girl'* had been named Elizabeth.

*

It was the only good news the *Gazette* could report, because by the time Elizabeth Jarvis was three months old, and by the time the *Surry* had reached England, a new song had entered Australian folklore.

Emancipists found that the government of Sir Thomas Brisbane had swiftly removed all the rights they had been given by Lachlan Macquarie.

Under the new *Transportation Act*, the emancipist land settlement policy was thrown out. All Pardons given by the former Governor were now invalid, as until a felon's name appeared in a General Pardon sealed with the Great Seal of England a felon had no rights at law.

Mr Justice Field, in Sydney's High Court, made the announcement that a Governor's Pardon, as distinct from a Royal Pardon, did not restore a convict to any civil rights, save the right to remain on earth.

And once again, convicts experienced the relentless lash of Botany Bay law.

Exclusives fumed as the emancipists in the towns and the convicts in their chain gangs, continually sang out their new protest song:

'Macquarie was a Prince of men!
Australia's pride and joy!
We ne'er shall see his like again!
Bring back our great Viceroy!'

PART FIVE

Chapter Thirty-Seven

Island of Mull
Scotland

The letter from Australia, when it eventually reached Gruline, was nine months old.

Lachlan read it carefully, then raised his eyes from the pages and gazed stonily out of the window. It was less than three years since he had left Australia, yet he knew with certainty that if he did not act quickly, it would be too late.

The window of his study looked out on green fields surrounded by woodlands. The setting was idyllic and there was no other place, according to Elizabeth, more restful on Earth.

The door flew open and his son came into the room, young and healthy and golden, full of life and vitality and impatience. 'Are you coming, Papa? If we don't go soon, there'll be no time to fish.'

Lachlan looked at his son, and smiled gently. Life was so short, yet for the young even a long summer's day was still not long enough for all the things they wanted to do.

'No fishing,' he said, 'not today. There are too many other things I need to do. Why not ask George to take you?'

'I'll ask George,' the boy agreed, and dashed off as if there was not a moment to waste.

282

A short time later, from the window, Lachlan saw his son and George Jarvis setting off together in the sunshine, saw the way they walked and talked companionably together, and suddenly Lachlan felt himself ravaged by a desolate sense of loss. Much worse than the ravaging pain that had been torturing his body for months.

He now knew that he would never experience the joy and fulfilment of seeing his son grow into manhood, but he had known and loved the boy for ten years, and he thanked God for even that.

Elizabeth walked in on him a few hours later, surrounded by a litter of his personal possessions. He had cleared out his desk and boxed up all his personal papers.

'What are you doing?' she asked in bewilderment. 'I thought you had gone fishing with Lachlan.'

Still silent, he pushed aside some papers on his desk and handed her the letter from Australia.

She took it and read it thoroughly, angry emotions moving over face, and then she looked at him. 'So what will you do? What *can* you do?'

'I can go to London. That's *all* I can do.'

When?'

'As soon as possible ... tomorrow morning.'

She was nodding, she understood and agreed with his motives for going to London immediately.

'But why all this?' She slowly looked around at the boxes on the floor. 'You are only going to London. Not back to Australia.'

He made a careless gesture with his hand. 'Oh, I was just in the mood, and I thought it was about time I sorted my papers into some sort of order, if only to help me find them more quickly when I need them.'

She gazed at him in silence. An insect was buzzing loudly in the quiet warmth of the room. 'You look tired,' she said. 'Are you sure you are well?'

'Oh, yes, I'm fine,' he assured her. 'Just, as you say, a little tired.'

'Then if you are intent on travelling to London tomorrow, you will have to make sure you are in bed early tonight. No more staying up to read a book into the small hours. Promise me that, you will, Lachlan, an early night, before your journey.'

'I promise.'

She stood looking at him for a moment, satisfied, knowing that was one thing he had never done – given his promise and then broken it.

And she also knew that his need now to go to London as soon as possible, was due to that last promise he had given to the people of Australia on the day he had left its shore.

When she had left the room he turned away to the window, realising he would have to take an extra dose of laudanum to prevent the pain from waking him – and Elizabeth – in the night.

He turned back into the room and sat down at his desk. Throughout his life, and especially in Australia, he had driven people hard, but never harder than he had driven himself. Through overwork he had strained his physical constitution, the doctor had said. And now he must pay the price.

But he still had one last battle to fight, and it had to be fought in London.

A battle with politicians.

'Politicians are not born, they are excreted,' Cicero had said. And that old First Consul of ancient Rome had known his politicians, Lachlan reflected wryly.

Many English politicians – men whose only personal knowledge of him was the tittle-tattle of his foes and the biased reports of Commisioner John Bigge, had spoken out against him and his government of New South Wales; but Lachlan knew that he still had many friends in high places. And on that alone, everything now depended.

*

He left Scotland at dawn the following morning, accompanied only by George Jarvis.

In London he took rooms at a hotel in St James, a distance of just a short walk to Whitehall's offices of power.

His old friends received him warmly, and although at times he felt almost giddy with sickness, he put on a cheerful face and accepted every social invitation and used every contact he had.

At the end of June he finally took his cause to

the Duke of York, who sat and listened seriously to his plea on behalf of the emancipists in Australia.

The following afternoon he was received by the King at Carlton House. It had been almost twenty years since those days when he had dined with Lord Harrington and the Prince of Wales – now George IV – but the King remembered him well.

They discussed the petition that the emancipists of New South Wales had sent to him, in the desperate hope that he would be able to personally present it to His Majesty.

The King slowly read the petition which had been signed by 1365 of — '*those persons by whose labour your Majesty's Colony has been cleared and cultivated, its towns built, its woods felled, its agriculture and commerce carried on. Yet your petitioners, retrospectively and prospectively, are to be considered as convicts attaint, without personal liberty, without property, without character or credit, without any one right or privilege belonging to free subjects.*

'Your Majesty,' Lachlan said, 'these emancipists believe it is wrong and unfair that despite a generation of good conduct and hard industry, they are now thrown back to a state of degradation from which they thought they had deservedly risen.'

The King looked thoughtful, and then distressed. He sighed indecisively, and then changed the subject altogether – to the happier subject of India. After all, India was now part of the Empire, a jewel in his crown, and the architecture of his magnificent Pavilion at Brighton had been inspired by the beauty and splendour of the Indian Pavilions.

Such was the wayward jollity of King George IV that Lachlan was almost cheery at the end of his visit, but he was none the wiser.

And then, finally, after weeks of endless meetings with senior politicians, Lachlan was officially informed by the Secretary of State, Sir Robert Peel, that a new clause was to be inserted into the *Transportation Act*, restoring to emancipists all their former rights and privileges – not only in Australia – but in all of His Majesty's dominions.

Lachlan returned to his hotel rooms in Duke Street, took up his pen and wrote a letter to his friends in New South Wales, giving them the good news. His last fight for his beloved Australians had been won. They had served their sentences, and paid their debt. Nothing more could be taken away from them now. Not now. The new clause had received the Royal Assent.

When he had signed the letter, he threw the pen from him and sat back in his chair, staring at the wall like a man who is staring at his whole life. He frowned – not at the stabbing pain, which he had become used to – but at the new and unexpected inner calm he suddenly felt.

George Jarvis came up behind him and put a hand gently on his shoulder. 'Come, you need to rest now. Let me help you to bed.'

Lachlan refused, and then changed his mind, deciding he would like a rest after all.

Once he was in bed and lying back on the pillows, his eyes closing in sleep, George stood looking at him for a long time, and then quietly left the room and sent a message post-haste to Elizabeth, telling her he believed she should come to London as quickly as possible.

Returning to the bedroom, George sat down on a chair by the bed, and lifted Lachlan's hand in his own.

Lachlan opened his eyes and looked back at George with an expression of extreme tenderness.

'George.'

'Yes, my father.'

'What will you do?'

'Whatever you ask me to do.'

'I have already asked so much of you ...' And then a dark shadow of sorrow came into Lachlan's eyes and he said anxiously,

'Eight months, George, eight months before they receive my letters in Sydney, eight months before they know about the Royal Assent to the restoration of their rights and dignity.'

George could not answer, because his heart was breaking. Even though he had known for weeks that Lachlan was dying, and had been sworn to secrecy, the reality of it now was almost beyond his endurance.

'But ... my son,' Lachlan went on worriedly.

'George ... he is only a child.'

'Don't worry,' George assured him quietly. 'I will take good care of him.'

'And Elizabeth?'

'And Elizabeth also.'

'Lord Strathallan is the executor of my Will, so he will become Lachlan's *legal* guardian, he will insist upon that. He will also see to the administration of the Jarvisfield estate on Elizabeth's behalf; but, George, I have also set up the *Macquarie Trust*, which is for you.'

'I don't want or need anything from you,' George replied. 'You know that.'

'Yes, I know that ... but who knows the future ...'

The tears were sliding down George's face. 'I have sent for Elizabeth ... and asked her to bring Lachlan with her ... you will see them both again, in just a few days.'

George held Lachlan's hand even tighter, as if silently telling him, '*so hang on, fight as you have always fought for everyone else, and hang on until they arrive ...*'

Lachlan smiled faintly. He knew what George was silently saying, and nodded. 'I understand, George ... I'll do my best.'

'You always do.'

And then an overwhelming sense of peace came over Lachlan as he looked into George's dark eyes. A feeling of trust and faith that he knew would never be broken. With George Jarvis there at Gruline, the boy would always have a man around, a man who truly loved him. A man who would help him in the ways that only another man can, a fine man.

Cool mind, clear judgement, warm heart. That was George Jarvis.

Lachlan closed his eyes and let his mind drift along a path of memories that led all the way back to that day in India when he had first set eyes on that small struggling slave-boy in the bazaar at Cochin ... It had been a long road from Cochin to here, a long road through long years, but it would be that same little slave-boy who, as a man, would take good care of his own little boy now.

He smiled to himself. Oh yes, as always, George Jarvis was right: 'Heaven's way always comes around.'

Epilogue

When the news of Lachlan Macquarie's death in London reached Australia, the bulk of the population of New South Wales went into mourning. Shops and houses put up their shutters for a week, and the *Gazette* draped its pages in black.

The church bells of St Philip's church tolled at dawn and at dusk for seven days. Emancipists met in sad groups in each other's houses. Old swags wept openly on roadways, and streams of young male and female convict servants joined the long silent procession through the shuttered town towards Sydney harbour where – at sunset on the seventh day, scarlet lines of soldiers stood with hands raised to their hats in silent salute as a bugler played *The Last Post*.

To a stranger arriving in Sydney, it must have seemed as if a monarch had died. But to the people, Lachlan Macquarie was more than merely a king. He was, and always would be, *'The Father of Australia.'*

> *'He was a perfect gentleman, and a supreme legislator of the human heart ... Whenever the sculptor shall imagine a guardian angel for New South Wales and Van Diemen's Land, the chisel of gratitude shall portray the beloved and*

majestic features of General Lachlan Macquarie.

Hobart Town Gazette, 1824

JARVISFIELD

A mixture of the Arabic blood of her father, and the English blood of her mother, Elizabeth (Beth) Jarvis grows up on the estate of Jarvisfield in Scotland. A dark-haired, dark-eyed girl of uncommon beauty who enslaves the hearts of two young men, while loving only one.

Lachlan Macquarie Junior, rich and golden, and the heir to his famous father's estate, is the joy of his mother's heart, until she finally realises that the only man her son is capable of respecting, and the only one who can control him, is Beth's father, George Jarvis.

Based on the true-life stories of the *Macquarie, Jarvis* and *Dewar* families, and set in the natural beauty of the Island of Mull, *JARVISFIELD* is a stand-alone novel in its own right, and the third book in *The Macquarie Series*.

Thank You

Thank you for taking the time to read *'The Far Horizon'* the second book in The Macquarie Series. I hope you enjoyed it.
Please be nice and leave a review.

*

I occasionally send out newsletters with details of new releases, or discount offers, or any other news I may have, although not so regularly to be intrusive, so if you wish to sign up to for my newsletters – go to my Website and click on the "Subscribe" Tab.

*

If you would like to follow me on **BookBub** go to:-
www.bookbub.com/profile/gretta-curran-browne and click on the "*Follow*" button.

Many thanks,

Gretta

www.grettacurranbrowne.com

Also by Gretta Curran Browne

MACQUARIE SERIES

BY EASTERN WINDOWS

THE FAR HORIZON

JARVISFIELD

THE WAYWARD SON

***

LORD BYRON SERIES

A STRANGE BEGINNING

A STRANGE WORLD

MAD, BAD, AND DELIGHTFUL TO KNOW

A RUNAWAY STAR

A MAN OF NO COUNTRY

ANOTHER KIND OF LIGHT

NO MOON AT MIDNIGHT

***

LIBERTY TRILOGY

TREAD SOFTLY ON MY DREAMS

FIRE ON THE HILL

A WORLD APART

***

ALL BECAUSE OF HER
A Novel
(Originally published as GHOSTS IN SUNLIGHT)

RELATIVE STRANGERS

(Tie-in Novel to TV series)

ORDINARY DECENT CRIMINAL
(Novel of Film starring Oscar-winner, Kevin Spacey)

Printed in Great Britain
by Amazon

38887663R00169